SWEET WELLS

Recent Titles by Elizabeth Gill from Severn House

THE FOXGLOVE TREE
THE HOMECOMING
HOME TO THE HIGH FELLS
THE PREACHER'S SON
THE SECRET
SILVER STREET
SWAN ISLAND
SWEET WELLS
WHEN DAY IS DONE
WHERE CURLEWS CRY

SWEET WELLS

Elizabeth Gill

This first world edition published 2008
in Great Britain and the USA by
SEVERN HOUSE PUBLISHERS LTD of
9–15 High Street, Sutton, Surrey, England, SM1 1DF.

British Library Cataloguing in Publication Data

Gill, Elizabeth, 1950-
Sweet Wells
1. Domestic fiction
I. Title
823.9'2[F]

ISBN-13: 978-0-7278-6675-2 (cased)

Except where actual historical events and characters are being described for the storyline of this novel, all situations in this publication are fictitious and any resemblance to living persons is purely coincidental.

All Severn House titles are printed on acid-free paper.

Printed and bound in Great Britain by
MPG Books Ltd., Bodmin, Cornwall.

For Diane Allen and Helen Bibby of Magna Books and Peter Douglas and Mark Merrill of Ulverscroft, for the people of County Durham who benefit from the Books On Wheels programme, and for everybody involved in the programme, many of whom give their services free so many can listen to audio books in their homes, take large print books from libraries and reap the benefit of Agatha Christie's insistence that everybody is entitled to have the enjoyment of books, one way or another. And thank you all for giving me such wonderful memories, such good times.

Prologue

1918

The snow was never bad in the city. Jonas Ward had to remind himself of this as he watched the big square flakes falling past his office window and turning the pavement white in the small city of Durham. It was much more low-lying than the Durham dale where his family had lived for generations.

The snow melted faster on narrow pavements than it ever did in the fields and on the tops of moors; it did not linger up the cobbled streets of the small city where the houses were often close at either side, old streets with tiny twisting back lanes. The River Wear ran in a loop around three sides, making the city a fortress in older times with the castle on its remaining side effectively keeping out the enemy, keeping the people inside safe.

It did not feel safe now to him; it felt like the snow he had seen which remained in the dale from December to April, when it hid behind the big grey stone walls right through until Easter and sometimes beyond.

He loved the city. He was the first of his family to live there though they had had an office there for many years. His family were solicitors, but they had always travelled back to the little town of Sweet Wells, close to Stanhope, as though the office here in Old Elvet was just an afterthought.

His older brother, Edgar, would have nothing to do with the office in the city. He hid in the dale with his lovely Scottish wife, taking care of the familiar safe petty legalities, whereas Jonas was more ambitious. He was determined to expand the business and had brought his bride here to live in the city.

He and Edgar had both come back from the war early because of wounds when hundreds of thousands of men had died in France. He had been first back with a bad leg which still gave him a slight limp but had probably saved his life. Edgar too had been invalided out. Bradley had never gone to war. His health had been delicate since he was a child. It was that bloody damned house, Jonas thought. The freezing winds up on the top which had left him with weak lungs. It was typical of him.

Jonas had been determined, having gone through so much, to lead the life he had so much wanted and had thought about it when it seemed to him that he would never come home.

Thinking about it now, he moved uneasily in his chair. Catherine was a girl from the hilltops; her family were tenants of a sheep farm way out from any town. She and her sister, Rose, had been brought up on five hundred acres of the kind of land where you could see nothing but tiny square fields and moorland for miles and miles.

Jonas and his friend Bradley Grant, who was an accountant, had met the girls at a dance in Stanhope and married them before the war. Bradley and his wife lived in the hills beyond Sweet Wells, in Bradley's family's huge country house, a bleak solitary place which was the very opposite of the house to which Jonas had brought Catherine, a pretty little terraced house in Hallgarth Street in the heart of the small city, and she was now seven months pregnant with their first child. Rose's baby was due soon.

Rose had written to beg her sister to return for the birth of her own child so Catherine had gone back to be there with her. As Catherine's baby was not due for another two months there was no reason why she should not go, and Jonas had not liked to argue with her, for fear she should think him selfish and unfeeling. Her family thought it bad enough she had left at all. For him to prevent her from returning on such an important occasion would have looked and sounded ill-natured at the least.

Though she had not said so, he knew that she had not taken to life in the city and had gone back to live with her parents when he was fighting in France. He blamed himself. It had been a dream that did not take wing, something that had existed only in his mind. A girl who was used to the moors could hardly be expected to enjoy the confines of a house which had nothing but a tiny lawn at the back. In fact she had stood out there the first spring that they were married and they had been happy and laughed over the rectangle of garden with the neat little hedges beyond their back door.

'Is this all the land we have?' she had said, and he had been obliged to tell her that he could afford nothing better.

His father would make him a partner in the practice later he felt sure, as he had with Edgar, but first he had to prove himself and his father was not given to the kind of generosity which would have bought them a fine house in the city. Everything was more expensive in town and his father, while glad at the idea of the business expanding, could not understand why Jonas should want to live there and had begrudged any money spent.

'There are plenty of specialist solicitors in Durham,' his father had said. 'Our speciality is in helping people we know.'

Jonas liked the city. He liked that the law courts and the prison were here as the very heart of the business in his eyes was criminal law. He had specialized in it and loved it. He was not interested in the kind of general practice his brother and father were involved in: the buying and selling of houses, the farmers' disputes, the petty squabbles that they sorted out, the legalities of the dying. He was tired of the neatness of it all, he had wanted more serious things and had got his way. Now, however, he got up from his suddenly uncomfortable chair and went to the window.

Old Elvet, the broad street which led to the courts and the prison, was covered in snow which was beginning to blow about with a cutting wind behind it. He could see by the way that the few passers-by shielded their faces with bowed heads, hats, and thick scarves. A wind like that would have had the farmers in Sweet Wells worrying about their livestock.

Jonas stood at his office window, waiting in vain for it to stop, thinking of his bed at home, his dinner and his fireside. They had only one maid; a young girl called Mary. She went home to her mother at the afternoon's end, to Atherton Street up by North Road, beyond the bus station, near the viaduct where the trains roared across the top.

He had taken her home the first couple of nights when he got there and since then had told her not to wait. He was always late, there was nothing to go home to and there was no reason why Mary should stay on. She would leave him his dinner on the side of the stove to reheat. She did her work well and in the winter it was not fair to keep her beyond dusk. He did not trust the city streets, especially the men who lingered outside the pubs and in dark corners. Mary was to go home in the daylight he insisted, though she protested that at this time of the year it was dark by four.

'Then go home at four,' Jonas had said.

'But, sir . . .'

'No buts,' Jonas said. 'Your mother would stop you coming at all if I didn't make sure you got back safely.'

This was true. Mary's mother had only let her daughter come to them on condition that she was not 'put upon' as she called it and Mary was too good at the household work and the cooking for him to consider losing her. She was at the moment all he had.

Twice he had written asking Catherine to come home. She had ignored his letters. He remembered the haste with which she had left him.

'My sister needs me,' she had said, pushing the letter under his nose, but he knew that she hungered for the dale.

He had grown jealous of her sister and of Bradley and the big grey stone Grant House where the Grants had lived apparently for ever. It was the nearest to the house the girls had known before they were married. Bradley came from a very old family, well established and respected, whereas Jonas's branch of the Wards were only third generation solicitors and it was nothing in the dale where some people had lived for a thousand years under the same name. His great-grandfather had been nothing but a farm labourer. Only in the dale, he thought, wincing, would people remember such things.

Jonas had wanted to move away from the clutching fingers of the small society where everybody knew everybody, talked about one another, watched and judged. He had seen Catherine and himself in the city going to dinner parties with city friends, enjoying musical evenings – he loved the violin.

He wanted to laugh at himself now. His wife had made no friends, and he could remember his disappointment right from the beginning as she had rebuffed the invitations they had had, either pretending she was busy doing something else or simply not returning an answer in time. She never went anywhere. The shopping was delivered, Mary did everything in the house, and the little back garden, rather than being somewhere Catherine would cultivate flowers and they could sit together on summer evenings, was a tiny jungle, the grass knee-high, the shrubs around it overgrown and the flower beds clogged with weeds.

He hated looking out on it and seeing its neglect, but when he had attempted to clear the weeds from the tiny beds, Catherine had sat by the window in the dusty living room as though she would stay for ever watching the road which led away from the city. He was convinced that she sat there hour after hour when he was at work and Mary scurried around doing everything so that he should not notice or think things were left undone. As if he cared any more.

He had thought that things would be different when he came home. He imagined she would have accustomed herself to being his wife by then, but the long partings had made things worse. Sometimes, he thought uncomfortably, she put up with his embraces, she endured him in the bedroom and that was all. It was a great grief to him that his wife tolerated his touch and nothing more.

He wished he didn't love her as it made him ashamed, but he loved her so much while he had the feeling she didn't overly care for him. How simple it would be if you could withdraw your feelings, take back the needs and his affection. His marriage had become a very lonely place. The trouble was that on his part he wanted to go on, convinced that it would get better. They would spend more time together when she came home, he would make more money, buy her pretty things and in return he hoped she would turn up her face for his kisses, something she hadn't done in years.

He was hoping the child would improve things. She had seemed pleased. It would be so different. He didn't care whether it was a girl or a boy as long as they could become a real family at last. He had been struggling for so long but even now, having been without him for so many months, Catherine had gone back to the dale as though she needed to be there no matter what the consequences were.

Darkness was falling. The fire in his office was down to its last embers and he must trudge his way home through the snow. The little house would be so uninviting with its black windows. Perhaps he would go to one of the pubs after he got home and find the company of other men. The snow would stop.

His father had reported that Rose's child was almost a fortnight old so soon Catherine would make her way back to him and all would be well. He admitted to himself finally that he could not manage without Catherine. He loved her too much and was afraid of his feelings for her.

He knew now that she did not love him, that she had married him because it was a good match and her parents had been pleased as they had nothing to give her, nothing to leave her. Perhaps they had even persuaded her into it. He had been too young, too naïve to know, and he wished he could stop loving her because he knew that she felt suffocated.

She would turn from him in bed and refuse to speak at the table when they had meals together. It made no difference; she was the love of his life and she always would be. She would come home, she would have their child and after that they would be a family, they would be happy.

* * *

The snow was worse now. There was nothing to stop it up here on the tops. It had snowed almost constantly for three days. It felt like a lot longer, it was beginning to feel like for ever.

At first Bradley Grant had been pleased, grateful somehow that winter had shown itself properly. After weeks of nothing but wind and rain and sleet the big white flakes had turned the fields into blankets, the hedges into cotton wool, the trees whitened so that the evenings were ghostly. The wind had made intricate shapes against the garden walls and even Rose had smiled and been glad.

Bradley resented Catherine being there. He felt pushed out and knew that Jonas, not long reunited with his wife, was unhappy in Durham by himself. Jonas would write and beg his wife to go back to Durham, but the two sisters would not be parted and if Catherine wanted to go back to her husband she never said so. Though perhaps she did not say so because Rose begged her so hard to stay on, said that she could not manage without her.

It began to snow harder. After two days Bradley could not get down the fields to work and there would have been little point as there was no way he could reach Stanhope, where his office lay, in such weather. He was almost happy sitting there by the fire, thinking of the two women and the child in the kitchen or in the bedroom, laughing together and making cakes in the afternoons and dinner for him later. But after four days he just wished the snow would stop, but it didn't. It got deeper and deeper.

That night Catherine went into labour. It was too early, he knew it was, he knew that he should get help, but by then the snow was so deep that he could not have got down the track without losing his way in the blizzard. There was no means of contacting the doctor even if he could have helped.

The child was not due for another two months. Telling himself this did not help. Rose's pain was hard to listen to, her voice was full of fear and despair. He wished that he could run away. His wife's white face betrayed her, even though she said it must be false labour, it would soon be better, the contractions would stop, they must stop. She sponged Catherine's face and neck but the contractions did not stop, the pain did not ease and the snow blew across the tops.

Rose came downstairs, moving softly as though any more noise might make things worse.

'She isn't getting any better. I don't think this is false labour. We must get help,' she said.

Bradley didn't want to panic her, he had been reassuring and she in her turn had tried to be confident but it had gone beyond that.

'We're going to have to manage,' he said, and he thought back to Rose's own labour. It had gone on for two days but she had been fine in the end. The doctor had been there, but he thought probably if they had had to they would have been all right. He remembered how he had spent most of those two days pacing up and down in the sitting room and that recollection was no help at all.

'I'm frightened,' his wife said.

'You mustn't let her know that.'

She went back upstairs. Bradley shut out the weather, pulled thick velvet curtains across the windows, built up the fires in the bedroom, in the living room, the stove in the kitchen. What help they had, a maid and a general labourer, had not turned in for three days and when he went outside, wondering whether there was any way in which he could get to the village in the storm he knew with a countryman's undeniable knowledge that he would never make it.

The drifts were as high as the house, the little town below was blotted out, the snow was blowing horizontally so that he could see nothing. He ventured beyond the door and straight into a drift so deep that he had difficulty in extricating himself from it. It would be of no help if he died on the way to the village, men had done so, been lost in such storms, not knowing their way, walking blind before the whiteness without direction.

He went back inside and reluctantly up the stairs, hoping vainly that Catherine would be better or that they would at least be able to deliver the child and relieve her of her burden. In the other room Rose's new daughter, Madeline, was silent. She was sleeping peacefully, but he still went across to her cot and checked. Her tiny round pink cheeks were perfect, her long eyelashes closed and her small fists clenched.

Somehow with the sounds of pain from one room and the silence from the other the house was full of suffering. There was to be no relief. The snow did not stop; he could not go for the doctor.

The baby was born, they did what they could but it was dead. Catherine sweated and burned all through the night, crying out for her child and then for her family. She imagined she was in Durham and wished and sighed for the house on the tops, for her parents, for the endless moor which was her home. She imagined it in August with the heather bright and the bees buzzing and the sunlight in the sky. She tried to get up and go outside to see the moors. Bradley had to stop her, to hold her as she panicked and fought, though she was too weak to leave her bed.

Even when he had extinguished the fire and let the room grow cold her face was shiny with heat and her body swollen as her ravings grew worse. She cried out hour after hour and he knew that he would never forget these terrible days and how Rose had stayed there with her, had not reacted even when the baby did not move. She said nothing to him, it was almost as though he did not exist, she talked to her sister, soothed and comforted, bathed her, held her, tried to calm her.

Catherine died the same afternoon. Rose was inconsolable. She finally broke down, begged of her sister not to leave her, kissed her all over her face long after Catherine had stopped breathing. Bradley said nothing, he stood by and waited for the grief to pass.

When the snow stopped there was still nothing he could do. He had to wait for three days until the sun had melted enough of it to allow him to wade down to the doctor's house in the village. He was exhausted, soaked, the snow had been up to his waist all the way. He did not want to go back there, he didn't ever want to go back and yet he could not linger by the doctor's fire while his wife was alone up at the house with her sister's body and the dead baby. His only comfort was to think of his child, it was all that had taken Rose from Catherine, the baby screaming in the other bedroom, the idea that she might neglect her child and even then he had had to coax her away.

William Robson, newly qualified, went with him back up the fields. His father had been called to an emergency in the village and could not go and, besides, the woman and the baby were dead. They did not need a doctor, they needed an undertaker.

William tried to tell him that there was nothing he could have done to prevent it, no way he could have helped, but Bradley could not accept this.

He stood his friend's calm words for as long as he could before saying, 'I was to blame, I should have sent her home before, but Rose wanted her here. She had such a bad time when the baby was born and—'

'The baby was not due for another two months. It had nothing to do with where she was.'

'If it hadn't been for her being here. If it hadn't been for the snow. If she had been in Durham . . .'

'Will you stop blaming yourself?' William said.

Bradley looked the width of the sitting room at him.

'You think Jonas isn't going to blame me?'

Catherine's husband was a hot-tempered young man and in love. He would need someone to blame.

'Things like this happen sometimes,' William said. 'No one can help it.'

Bradley held those words against himself when he went to bed. The following day he wished very much that William had been at the house when Jonas got there.

Jonas didn't even speak as he pushed past Bradley at the door, took the stairs rapidly and burst into every room until he found the room where his dead wife and child lay. The door slammed and then there was silence. Bradley didn't think he could bear to wait through the silence for Jonas's wrath, but he had no choice.

He waited next to Rose with the baby in her arms – he would have liked to suggest to her that she not be there or at least the child not be there, but he couldn't – by the fire that dreadful afternoon while there was no noise from above. It went on hour after hour until he finally heard the footsteps on the stairs and Jonas came into the room. He thrust shut the door.

'Why didn't you send her home to me?'

'She didn't want to go,' Bradley said.

'You should have sent her. She was my wife, I needed her. She was supposed to be living with me. You knew how things were.'

Rose hid against her baby's shawl. She had gone through enough, she shouldn't have to put up with this, Bradley knew. She had lost her beloved sister and their relationship, he acknowledged now with pain, was a closer one than they had had with either of their husbands.

'I wanted Catherine here,' Rose said. 'I wanted my sister near me. I'm sorry.'

'Sorry?' Jonas glared at her. 'You two and this bloody house have cost me my wife and child. Didn't you ever think about her?'

'She wanted to be here,' Rose said.

'Rose, don't argue with Jonas.' Bradley knew it was pointless. Jonas was wild with grief. 'It's true,' Bradley said, in spite of what he had said to his wife about not arguing. He couldn't help himself, Jonas was so misguided. He shouldn't blame them for what had happened. 'She hated Durham, she was a lass off the hilltops, why shouldn't she? You took her to live in a little terraced house on a busy street, it was like a prison to her.'

'So this is my fault?' Jonas glared at him and Bradley was afraid.

'It was nobody's fault. How can you say such things?' he said, becoming angry himself though trying not to. He felt guilty enough as it was. Jonas was only making things worse.

Jonas started shouting at him, saying unjust things which Bradley did not listen to. He had had enough.

'Why don't you go, while there's still enough light to see you down the road? I don't want you here.'

Jonas turned on him.

'You and your stupid bloody house. If this had been in a civilized place she could have been helped, she could still be alive. You encouraged her to come here, to stay here, to leave me.'

'It's nothing to do with the house,' Bradley said. 'She'd had enough of city life, you knew that. You should have come home and brought her with you. It was all she wanted.'

Bradley took his wife into his arms as she began to weep over the unjustness of Jonas's accusations. He was lucky that he still had his wife and child. The young man with the appalled dark eyes had nothing left and Bradley would never forgive himself for being part of it or forget that dreadful night when Catherine had sweated and moaned and given birth and burned up. It was as though she had burned out of existence while the snow suffocated the house until the very ground outside was silent.

'I want you to go now,' Bradley said.

'I'll see my day with you. Just wait,' Jonas threatened.

'If it's easier for you to blame people then go ahead. There's nothing more we can do.'

Jonas slammed from the house. He did not come back. He did not come back for his wife and child's funeral. He did not come back to his father's house or to see his brother. Bradley did not see him again. Rose was left to bury her sister and the child, to put up a stone, to walk to the grave-side each Sunday when they went to church. Jonas did not come back and they were left to mourn.

1930

Jonas was not eager to see Bradley Grant that afternoon. He would not have been eager to see him any afternoon, he acknowledged to himself. He had never been able to go back, his stupid pride had stopped him. It was too late now, he knew it was. He had behaved so very badly and Bradley and Rose had been so stupid and he had tried to forgive them all but he couldn't.

He had let Bradley find him. Bradley had gone to Edgar, Jonas's elder brother who was the solicitor in Sweet Wells, and Edgar had gone to Wilton Marlowe whom he had suspected was Jonas's solicitor in various places but obviously in Durham so that people might know how to contact Jonas, and Wilton had come to Jonas.

Jonas and Bradley met at the County Hotel on the riverside in Old Elvet in Durham. It brought back many difficult memories. Jonas had not been there since his young wife had died, but in Durham, strangely, he could be anonymous. He didn't know anybody any more and he had been able to avoid the street where he and Catherine had lived briefly and the office in the city which Edgar now owned but did not run. Edgar, Jonas thought with disgust, was still a dale man, had never grown, never reached out, never done anything interesting or worthwhile. He was tied to that dreadful little town where they had been born.

Jonas didn't want anybody anywhere near his own work. He didn't want people to know what he was doing. The less contact he had with anybody from the dale the better, but he had agreed to meet Bradley in a private room at the County and when Bradley walked in Jonas was shocked. He had altered in that time, he looked much older than he was.

'Hello, Jonas.' Bradley didn't even offer to shake hands. He didn't sit down and Jonas didn't ask him to.

'What is it?' he said.

'I need a favour.'

It made Jonas laugh.

'Your sense of humour was always your biggest failing,' he said.

Bradley sat down so that the conversation would not be overheard. He could not know that Jonas had hired the room, that the door had been shut behind Bradley and they would not be interrupted until Jonas said so. He sat on the sofa opposite, on the very front of it, but before he had chance to say anything Jonas said, 'How is your family?'

'Very well.'

Jonas looked at him. Bradley, like Edgar, had never got away. He pitied them.

'And Rose?'

'She's fine.'

'Do you have sons?'

'Only a daughter.'

'Just one?'

'Only the one, yes. Do you – do you have any children?'

'No.'

'You could have married again.'

'Good heavens, yes. Have you any idea how many times people have said so, as though everyone can be replaced.'

'It doesn't have to be like that.'

'How in the hell would you know? What is it, Bradley? What do you lack?'

'Money. Doesn't everything boil down to that?'

'Not in my experience, but then our paths haven't crossed so I have no idea what your life has been like. You need to borrow some? Why don't you go to a bank?'

'I did. Now they want it back. I cannot tell Rose.'

'Ah, the joys of the married life. Keeping secrets from one's wife. How much?'

Bradley mentioned the figure. Jonas looked at him.

Bradley hesitated and then he said, 'The bank will take my house and . . . I'm not well, I can't work any more. It costs so much to keep up, it's always been a very expensive place—'

'It's always been a bloody Godforsaken place!'

'It's our home and there hasn't been enough money to keep it as it should be kept for a very long time.'

'Yes, I remember,' Jonas said. 'Insular little villages, people who think the outside world is a trip to Darlington, the sing-song voice of the dale, the stagnant ideas of the uneducated.'

'I understand you have made a lot of money.'

'Tragedy concentrates the mind wonderfully, you know. How will you ever pay it back?'

'I don't know yet.'

'So I shall have the deeds to the house and if you can't pay it back I shall have the house itself and if it comes to it you will leave, you and your family.'

Bradley said nothing.

'You weren't expecting more, surely?' Jonas got up. 'You can give my brother the details. He can sort it out. No one is to know. If you tell anyone—'

'Rose must know.'

'Nobody,' Jonas said again. 'If it becomes scandal in the area I will hear about it and I will make sure that you are put from your house straight away. Do feel free to stay here, the room is hired for the rest of the afternoon.' With that Jonas walked out.

He went home. He had never been as glad to go anywhere, his lovely stone house in Northumberland within sound of the sea, within reach of his work where the pit wheels turned day and night. His house stood in a dozen acres with formal gardens around it and the edge of his land was on the seafront which you could see clearly from the bedrooms.

Mary heard him clash the front door. She came into the hall. They had been together since the very night he had come home after his wife had died. He could hardly bear to think about it now.

That night she had waited for him to return and he had clashed the door much as he had just done now and had said wearily, 'You should have gone home. How many more times do I have to tell you?'

She had said nothing. Jonas had made his way into the little front room which his wife had disliked so much because passers-by could see in. She had put up net curtains at the windows, but you could hear people even now in the darkness of the late evening, their footfalls, their quiet conversation. Somebody even laughed.

There Jonas broke down. He knew that he shouldn't, he knew it was a disgusting weakness in men and that he had made a mess of everything and that he should never have married Catherine, never have taken her away. It was nothing to do with Bradley and Rose, it was his own ridiculously stupid fault. He had let his bodily urges overcome his common sense. He had wanted her so much and when he had married her he had provided a cell for her here. He couldn't stop crying, the bleakness of coming back here had been too much for his self-control. Was he to be left to these few rooms and his guilty conscience?

He had not been aware of Mary being in the room until she had come over to him and got hold of him. He tried to shake her off, gently because there was no reason she should put up with him behaving like that. She retreated only a couple of feet.

'I'll take you home. I won't need you any more,' he said.

'Tell me what happened.'

'She's dead. Catherine's dead and my child.'

'Oh, Mr Ward, I'm that sorry.'

'It's all right. I'll be all right. It's nothing to do with you anyway. You've been very good. I won't need you here now.'

'What are you going to do?'

He didn't look at her.

'I don't know. Go away somewhere, I expect, anywhere away from here, away from the places that remind me of her.' He turned from Mary and was even more ashamed now that he had stopped crying that he had actually done so in the first place.

'I'm not going home,' Mary said.

He had never heard her use that tone before; her voice was authoritative rather than the polite almost deferential tone she usually used to him.

'I'm staying here with you,' she said.

'You can't. It isn't respectable. Your mother would take me to task if you stayed even an hour alone here with me.'

Mary nodded.

'I didn't tell her Mrs Ward hasn't been here at all lately and I've been running the house. I like running your house, it's the best my life's ever been. I think your house is so pretty.'

'I'll be selling it,' he said.

'Oh, don't do that,' Mary said. 'And please don't make me go home, I don't like it there. Let me stay here with you.'

'You can't. I said. It isn't right.'

'We could make it right.' She came to him and kissed him.

He was astonished.

'Mary, I'm sorry. You just feel sorry for me.'

'Aye, I do,' she said, 'but it hasn't stopped me from wishing I was Mrs Ward all this time.' She kissed him again. It was a very good kiss. Jonas hadn't had a very good kiss in as long as he could remember. Whatever his wife had been to him, he thought now and possibly because he was out of his mind, it was totally clear she had never been his lover.

Jonas tried to stop her but only with words. He couldn't manage any more, he was exhausted.

'I don't want you. I don't want you here.'

'Yes, you do,' she said in her newly confident voice.

Mary kissed him all over his face and when she had done that he could feel her young body against him and that she was willing. He pulled her clothes off and had her on the sofa as though another thing to be ashamed of didn't really matter any more.

He had not known how hungry he was, it had been such a long time since Catherine had given herself freely like this, in fact he wasn't sure she had ever done it. She had been so naïve when they met, when they married, she knew nothing, nobody had told her anything. He thought she had been so shocked by the process she had never got over it.

He and Mary went to bed and there Jonas had her until he could scarcely move. He kept waiting for her to protest, to turn away, to deny him, but she didn't, she encouraged him, wanted him, her body yielding in his arms as he had so much wanted Catherine to yield and then she had held him and touched him as his wife never had. They had hugged one another close and finally slept.

It was only in the morning, when the light put tentative fingers around the curtains, that he ventured with some semblance of humour, 'Your father will kill me. I won't have to worry about anything.'

'He certainly will,' Mary said. 'We need to get away.'

'Where?'

'Oh, anywhere my father won't find us.'

'You will come with me then?'

'Too true,' Mary said flatly.

'Look, I don't know that I will ever care about anybody again.'

'You will.'

'Does it matter?'

'No, I just want to go with you. I'll take now. We'll worry about the future when we get there. Let's be off before anybody finds out.'

She got up and packed two bags and that was the last time Jonas had been in Durham before he returned to meet with Bradley.

When he got back to his fine house there she was waiting in the hall. She took him into her arms, he didn't need to say anything, he had told her where he was going and although he could be tough at work and resilient in front of Bradley, in front of any man, he didn't need to do it here and it was such a relief. Mary knew all his secrets, all his needs. He could acknowledge to himself now that she loved him as Catherine had not and that he loved her differently than he had loved his wife and in many ways it was better.

They went in by the fire and he told her about the house.

'I don't think any good will ever come from that place,' she said. 'You should pull it down, or let it fall down. It's cursed.'

'You don't really believe in such things.'

'There are places that are evil just as there are men that are evil.'

'You're trying to make me feel better,' he accused her.

'Don't I always?' and she smiled up into his eyes and kissed him.

'Why won't you marry me?'

'Because there's only been one Mrs Ward and I don't care to compete.'

She was so confident these days, he thought with satisfaction, so well spoken, so dear to him. He was always a little bit afraid that she would leave him. She said she never would, but she maintained a spark in her eyes and though it was one of the things he liked best, he was never sure of her. She might not have chosen to be his wife, but she was certainly his friend and his lover and he thought that was best of all.

'Do you think I shouldn't have offered to buy it?' he said. She was the only person he ever asked advice from.

Mary hesitated.

'What?' he said.

She still hesitated.

'Tell me.'

She looked clearly at him. She never lied. And even if she thought he would find the truth unpalatable she always gave it to him.

'Do you still think of Catherine dying there?'

'I suppose I always shall, but I don't regret us, I shall never regret it. I love you, Mary.'

'Well, then,' she said lightly, 'if you thought it was a good idea to buy it from him you were doing him a favour even if he didn't know it. He would have lost it.'

'He will lose it. I don't know how long he will live, but I wouldn't give him more than a few years.'

'And then it will be yours. What will you do with it?'

'I shall let it fall down and nobody will ever be stuck there in the bloody snow ever again.'

Mary kissed him and they went off into the dining room together to have supper.

One

1935

Her home was the most beautiful place in the whole world. Madeline Grant was sure of that. It looked down on the village of Sweet Wells as though it knew its place in life, it looked down on everything. The wind went screaming across the tops and the Grant House stood there as if it had been there for ever: big, bold, long, high with many windows which on a rare sunny day the gleaming light caught and held.

It had been there since the early 1800s with three storeys and the dwellings which had preceded it were tumbling down in wild and lovely disarray around it: a tall fourteenth-century part with high walls and windows like slits missing its roof and an eleventh-century part with two storeys and an outline of fireplaces where the birds loved to nest, with steps up the outside.

People said that when Border Reivers roamed the land and came down the hills from Rookhope, in the days of Rowland Emerson and George Carrick and the Rookhope Ryde, the Grants had run into the upper storey of their bastle house and remained there until the danger was past. No one knew how long the land had been owned by the Grants, but people had looked down from it possibly for more than a thousand years and marvelled at the beauty of the bleak landscape where the heather shielded the sheep from low winds in winter.

In the valley the River Wear ran clear and grey in the very bottom of the fields, and all up and down the valley a criss-cross of neat stone walls made the whole dale into a sort of quilt. The hills rose blue against the skyline in the mornings and set above the fields, the sheep and the odd tree, which stood out in the evenings.

Rookhope and Eastgate and Sweet Wells were all villages in Weardale around the small town of Stanhope. Sweet Wells was named for the gulleys at the bottom of the fields which the icy streams from the top fells ran into and the cattle loved to drink from because the water was so pure.

Around the village there were farms and big houses, some alongside the river, some just further up on the roadside, some halfway up the hills and one or two dotted along the skyline on the very tops where the fells began.

This was where Maddy's home was. You could see it across the tops for miles, stone-built, proud, big, almost arrogant looking, watching the Grants through the generations, providing shelter and warmth for them and theirs. Sometimes she thought it would be there for ever for them and it was such a comforting thought.

Sweet Wells was the kind of town which had a parish church, three chapels, several hotels – some of them had been temperance in the old days when there was lead mining in the area – and a dozen shops.

The houses clustered around the square in the centre and there was a main road which went to Durham one way and across to Tynedale the other, and there were various streets of houses which straggled along the edge of the town. At the back of the town the houses ran down to the River Wear, which wound its way down the dale to Durham and finally into the sea at the east of the county where Sunderland and its surrounding towns lay. Unless your business was farming or trading or some kind of quarrying there wasn't a great deal else to do in the dale.

It was one of those days when you wished you lived in the village. It was November and it was Saturday so they were at home. During the week and very often on weekends Maddy walked down to the village to take care of two old ladies, sisters, Miss Dora Robson and Miss Phyllis who needed somebody to help with their correspondence and to take them to see friends in the afternoons. They had help with cooking and cleaning, but Maddy would take them shopping and aid them with their needlework since they could no longer see very well. They told her tales of when they were young and would ride up the hill to her house to weekend parties.

'We had grey ponies,' Miss Dora had reminisced.

Today, however, her mother had wanted her to stay at home. The sleet was dark grey across the tops, the house had been shadowed all day.

Maddy's father was lying in bed in the room above where she sat huddled by the fire. She had heard the doctor say, 'He's in a bad way, Rose.'

The doctor did not usually speak in such a familiar way to her mother in front of other people so Maddy had stood in the hall, holding her breath for fear that they might hear her. She had not come out deliberately to listen to their conversation, but she had been locking up the hens before it got dark and was going through the hall to get back to the sitting room as quickly as possible. The kitchen was warm, the hall was not and bitter draughts swept through the house in such weather because there was nothing to stop it.

Dr Robson had known her mother since they had been small children, but he would still address her correctly as Mrs Grant. Today he called her Rose, thinking they were alone, his voice soft and sympathetic.

'I know.' Her mother's voice broke then as though the two words were all she could get out.

Maddy didn't move.

'I'll come back later.'

'You needn't.'

'I will.'

'I'll manage. You can't walk all the way up here in the dark in this kind of weather. It's not fit for a dog. I don't think there's much more you can do.'

'I can be here.'

'No, don't. You know he won't last the night.'

Maddy took in her breath and the doctor paused because he did not say to people such definite things, he would not commit himself even to old friends.

After a pause the doctor's feet sounded heavily on the stairs and Maddy dashed into the sitting room, closing the door, hoping the stairs, creaking beneath his weight, would hide any noise she made.

Maddy had blue eyes and red hair, like her Great Aunty Sarah who had gone to Australia when she was young and never been heard of since. It was the scandal of the family, she had been 'wayward'. It wasn't good to be wayward so Maddy didn't relish her looks, she would much rather have looked like her mother or her father especially somehow now. She thought it would have been a comfort to her parents.

She waited. She could hear the sound of voices, though not the words as the house had thick walls and heavy doors, at least the part of it where she and her mother lived. Voices would float away up to the top storey which was just attics and freezing cold most of the year round so they didn't go up there, it was used for storage and they used only three of the bedrooms on the floor below.

The villagers said the house was haunted. It was nothing of the sort, Maddy knew, but there were wide halls and high ceilings and shadows which moved in the wind. She knew they were caused by the trees outside but perhaps it had to do with the way that the Grants had lived here seemingly for ever. She could not be afraid of her ancestors.

She waited for what seemed like a very long time. The voices died away. Her mother was probably seeing Dr Robson to the gate. Did she call him William when they were alone? The men in the Robson family were always called William.

The door finally opened and her mother came in. She hesitated, the cold draught came with her.

'Your father is very ill,' she said. 'Do you want to go up and say goodbye to him?'

Maddy wanted to say no. She hadn't seen anybody dying. She didn't want to be involved; maybe her father would actually die while she was there and she didn't want to think about it.

Her mother, seeing her face, said kindly, 'You don't have to.'

'I must.'

The stairs were wide and sweeping as though they had been made for women in elegant dresses who were about to make an entrance in the hall below.

There was no carpet on the stairs nor had been for a long time. The carpet had grown so threadbare that it threatened to trip people up, and her mother, in fear that somebody should fall down the stairs, had had it taken up and thrown out so as Maddy walked up them the sound of her feet on the bare wood echoed through the house.

The door to her father's bedroom was closed as it had been for weeks against the cold of the rest of the house. She had been tiptoeing past recently because any sound disturbed his sleep. But now she opened it softly and went in.

A fire burned in the big grate. Some days the only time she had seen him was when she took wood upstairs to keep the fire burning and it took a lot of replenishing. She didn't begrudge it. It was a small thing to do for him and she was glad of anything she could do to help. At first he had wanted her there, sitting on the bed talking to him, or in the chair by the fire reading while he closed his eyes, but for some weeks now he dozed constantly and she would creep in with the wood and creep out again.

Her mother nursed him and Dr Robson came often. Her father did not complain. He had never been the kind of man who complained about anything. Other men might have objected to having a daughter and no son, but if it occurred to him to mind he did her the courtesy of not saying so.

The big double bed, which their mother had not shared with him for several months now – she slept in another room quite alone which Maddy thought must have been awful for her – stood by the window. He liked it so. He wanted to be able to look out at the fell beyond the house and Maddy knew, though nobody had voiced the idea, that her father would want to die looking at the fells. She didn't blame him for that. If you had to die, it was the only way to do it.

The curtains were pushed way back like the fells were

ready to receive him, were ready to take his spirit. Could you really stay there for ever, she wondered hopefully? Like your time here was just a journey and you belonged out there in the cutting wind and the darkness, where the wind wuthered through the heather, when the sheep grouped behind the wall for warmth and in the early mornings pheasants walked across the cold grass in all their glittering gold and brown finery. It would not be so bad, she thought, if you could do that.

Her father did not look as if he were going anywhere. He smiled, opened his eyes, said her name, held out his hand and called her 'my dear girl' just as he always did. She was almost reassured except that he was pale and thin. Her mother followed her into the room, but Maddy went to her father and leaned over and hugged him.

It was all a mistake, Maddy thought with gladness. He would get better, he would be there to smile at them forever and ever and then he closed his eyes as though the effort of them being in the room had exhausted him. Her mother smiled at her to go out and she did, closing the door carefully behind her.

Two

Maddy's father's funeral was over, he had been laid to rest in the old graveyard which extended right around the church and she felt comfortable about that because it meant that he was not far away. All the Grants were buried in that particular plot. Some of them had big marble graves and tall gravestones.

There had been a funeral tea in the village hall. It was too far for many of the older people to walk up the long narrow road all the way to the top where their house stood so Maddy had handed around cups and saucers and plates full of sandwiches and little cakes at the hall. She had been glad for something to do because everybody looked so sorrowful, her father had been well liked, her mother was well liked.

The church had been packed, and she knew the vicar, Mr Philips would be pleased by that. He hated having an empty church. Sometimes in the winter on Sundays she would have preferred to stay at home by the fire, but she hated the idea of Mr Philips at the morning service having nobody to give his sermon to.

He gave short sermons. Not the kind where your feet went to sleep because you had to sit still for so long or where you were reduced to looking about you for amusement. She had experienced those kinds when other clergymen came to preach or on the few times she had been to other churches.

Mr Philips' sermons were always to do with real things, about people and special occasions, and they were always what her mother called 'uplifting'. When you left the church not only did you feel better for going, but you could walk up the hill with a lighter step somehow.

So unless the weather was so bad that you could not see past the rain, hail, sleet or snow they turned out every week, and she was always glad she did because Mr Philips was that best of spiritual leaders, so her mother said, he always made you feel glad you were there, better that you had gone and that was what religion was meant to be about.

It was said that his wife thought he would become a bishop in time. She was always having people to the house for meetings, taking in tramps and helping out poor families, and doing everything she could to better their lot, but she was well liked too because she did so much for the community. There were always church bazaars and jumble sales and sewing groups and she ran the Sunday school.

After church Maddy and her mother would walk back up the hill and then they would make the Sunday dinner and it was always the best meal of the week.

Coming back up the hill, having left her father in the graveyard, Maddy did not feel any better, until she saw the house. Somehow when you saw it you always felt revived. She could not wait to get there, like the house was opening its arms to her. She felt like it was the only thing left.

Rose was concerned. Edgar Ward, the solicitor, had caught up with her at the village hall. He did not look at her. Edgar had not looked at anybody, Rose thought, in years. He did not say how sorry he was that Bradley had died even though they had known one another all their lives. All he said was, 'I need to see you. Can you come to the office tomorrow morning at about eleven?'

She glanced around. He had chosen his moment well, there was nobody near.

'I have my husband's will. There's nothing relevant, nothing left . . .'

'It isn't about that,' Edgar said, and at that moment Phoebe Robson, the doctor's wife, descended on her with a cup of tea.

'Eleven o'clock?' Edgar said.

'Come and sit down,' Phoebe said. 'You've had to deal with quite enough.'

* * *

Rose worried all night. She had discovered that when tragedy fell it did not stop other problems from occurring, rather it made them worse. It must be something to do with Bradley's death, otherwise why would Edgar want to see her. She said nothing to Maddy, there was no point in worrying her, she had had sufficient to contend with. The house was cold. She listened to the wind. Finally somehow it soothed her and sent her to sleep before dawn.

Edgar's office was one of the bleakest places she had ever seen. It sat on the end of his house, not the end that was the end terrace but on the other end next to another house, and it had tiny windows. His house was on the edge of the square and was modest for a successful solicitor but she assumed he liked living there because it meant everybody could get to his office without effort. He had many clients because people knew that the Wards had a good reputation for dealing fairly with everyone and they knew Edgar would do his best for them. He had a reputation for being knowledgeable and trustworthy.

He kept her waiting for fifteen minutes in the gloomy reception area; it was one of the longest fifteen minutes of her life. The cold wind cut under the door and against her ankles, and the furniture, which was old and no doubt valuable, made the place look even darker. It seemed so big and clumsy and ancient and had been there for as long as she could remember.

Ushered in by his clerk, she sat down across the desk from Edgar, who looked over it at her. He had a long, thin, narrow face with deep lines – it reminded her of a blood hound – and if his expression was anything to go by he had nothing good to tell her. His office, though large, was just as gloomy as the room outside. No fire burned in the grate, it was uncomfortably cold and there were big ledgers piled everywhere as though Edgar was very overworked.

The floors were bare linoleum, and although at one time the marble fireplace must have been beautiful, it was now cracked, its grate was empty, and the lovely green and white tiles on the floor around it were dusty and broken.

The chair creaked under her weight as though its legs had been holding up stout farmers for too long. It was stuffed with horsehair or something equally as uncomfortable. No doubt Edgar did not want his clients to stay for any longer than was necessary.

She wished he would at least give her a cup of tea, but Edgar was known to be mean. She presumed he was worth a lot of money, but he never seemed to spend any, did not go drinking or merrymaking, worked all the time. People said the lights burned in his office well beyond midnight and all day on Sundays. Some people did not agree with working on Sundays.

Edgar had a child, a boy, who was rarely at home. He was as old as Maddy but went to boarding school and seemed to spend his holidays elsewhere. Rose continued trying to think about anything but what she was there for. It had to be bad news and she wanted to delay it for as long as she could, though she was curious whether anything could be worse than what had already occurred. She doubted it. She tried to look straight across at Edgar and keep the concern from her face.

'Mrs Grant, let me tell you how sorry I am for your loss.'

'Thank you.' She was resolved to be patient. They had all been friends once, but it was a very long time ago and if he chose not to remember it or her first name then she did not want to particularly either.

'Are you aware that your house does not belong to you?'

Rose stared. What on earth was the man talking about? The house on the tops had always belonged to the Grants, it was their home. She had determined that whatever else happened she would never leave it. She and Maddy would work all their lives if they had to.

She had daydreams of her daughter marrying well and bringing a husband to live there and having children and carrying on the tradition of the family. Of late her daydreams had been few; her waking life was a nightmare.

Sleep was her only escape but it came to her only in small snatches so that she was never fully awake any more. Bradley had been ill on and off for years and she liked to be around for him always. She was perpetually tired but had become used to it so now she thought that her foggy mind was betraying her and her hearing.

'What do you mean?'

'My brother Jonas owns it.'

Rose wanted to stop staring, her upbringing still informing her that it was rude, but she couldn't. Edgar went on. 'I have had a letter from him after I wrote telling him that Bradley had died. He wants you to leave as soon as you can.'

'Your brother owns my house? Jonas? Are you being funny, Edgar?'

If Edgar Ward could have looked further down she had no doubt he would have done so.

'Bradley sold it to him . . . otherwise you would have run out of money a very long time ago.'

'He sold our house to your brother and didn't tell me? How on earth could he have done such a thing? The Grants have always lived there. It's their home, their . . . their piece of earth. Nobody else could own it. The whole idea is ridiculous.'

'He owed the bank a great deal of money. Jonas bought the house from him and made it possible for you to go on living there. Otherwise you would have lost it a very long time ago. Bradley knew how ill he was. He wanted to hold on to things as long as he could.'

'The bank?'

Edgar looked patiently at her.

'For a number of years now you have had nothing, isn't that so?'

'Bradley couldn't work.'

'He was already in debt when you married him. His father was in debt. It goes back a long way.'

An even more terrifying thought made its sickening way through Rose's brain.

'Am – am I in debt?'

'No. Jonas took care of it all. I'm not sure it was worth his while financially, in fact I'm sure it wasn't. It sounds awful to say it but in a way he saved you and your family from being put out of your home.'

'So why can't we live there now?'

Edgar said nothing for what felt to Rose like hours.

'That was part of the deal, that you would leave when Bradley died.'

'Why didn't Bradley tell me?'

'That was part of the deal too,' Edgar said.

'There must be something I can do,' Rose said.

'There is nothing legal which would be of any help to you. That is all I know. He owns it and although you could attempt to stay there I wouldn't if I were you. Jonas is a rich, powerful and very bitter man and he doesn't want you there. I wouldn't put it past him to throw you and all your possessions outside.'

'How could he put Bradley's wife and child out on to the street? Where does he think we can go?'

'That's not his concern.'

'He doesn't care.'

Edgar didn't answer. Rose had gone cold with shock and had a terrible desire to burst into tears, but her common sense told her it wouldn't do any good.

'He blamed me,' she said, 'when Catherine and the baby died. He thought it was my fault. And Bradley's. In that case why didn't he put us out straight away? What a terrible vindictive way to behave. Do you have his address? I must go and see him . . .'

Her voice trailed away. Edgar was shaking his head.

'It won't do you any good. I've had his specific instructions. I am to tell you that you must leave as soon as you can. You have a month.'

'A month? What am I to do in a month?' Rose had to hold her lips firmly together somehow to stay the tears. 'He was a nasty, hard, unfeeling young man with a ruthless ambitious streak a mile wide. I thought Catherine might be the saving of him.'

'I think she was for a while.'

'And after she died he went to the bad. I knew he would.'

'I doubt anything would have saved Jonas,' Edgar said. 'He was always wilful and difficult.'

'How could things have become so bad?' Rose said.

'If I remember correctly Bradley's father and his father before him couldn't afford the place either. It was an albatross, a stone around their necks. It cost so much to run that it emptied the coffers of the Grant family.'

It took Rose some time to recover from all this. She couldn't speak for shock and dismay. It was as though she had never known her husband. How could he have kept such a thing from her?

If he had told her maybe they could have organized somewhere else to go, done something useful, profitable and then she couldn't think what and she realized that Bradley would never have left, no matter how bad things got and that was why he had gone to his enemy.

He would rather risk Jonas's triumph and his own disaster than leave the house he loved. For the first time she was angry with her husband. He had known what would happen after he died and he had said nothing. He had left her to face her fate alone.

She wished Edgar had been more sympathetic, offered her some kind of help or at least a few minutes of his time so that she could have had time to collect her wits. She couldn't think. And she could sense already that he wanted her out of his office; that his next appointment would be sitting in his horrible dark and freezing little room outside. It was a miserable place, she thought, glaring at the black and empty fireplace, and Edgar was almost as bad as his brother.

And then a thought occurred to her. If Jonas had a family perhaps he might take a sympathetic view if she could appeal to him, to what better nature he must have.

'Is Jonas married? Does he—?'

'I know nothing about him, not even where he is. I deal with him through a third party. We never see one another, and he has never made any contact directly either with me or with any other members of our family. He lives in the Borders and makes a great deal of money and that's all I know. I cannot tell you the name of the third party, I'm not allowed. If I were you I would make arrangements to leave as soon as you can. There is nothing to be gained from delay. You have four weeks. After that he will send the bailiffs in, you can be sure. Now if you wouldn't mind . . .'

'And where am I supposed to go?'

Edgar didn't answer and Rose thought that she had never liked him. In fact she had never liked either of the Ward boys. He offered her no consolation, no help, and he just sat there, saying nothing, until she was obliged to get up on her shaking legs which would barely hold her upright.

When she came out of his office the winter sunshine blinded her. She wanted to cry but could not as she was in the main square. She bolted for Phoebe Robson's house down the hill not far from the river; a pretty low stone building with a wonderful garden at back and front, which she knew from having spent afternoons there eating cake and drinking tea in the fine weather before Bradley had been so ill that she couldn't leave him.

She thought back fondly in Phoebe's front garden as she banged on the door. Phoebe would help her and Will too. Phoebe opened the door and looked surprised but not quite pleased to see her.

'I'm just about to go out,' Phoebe said, and she was, all ready for the town, wearing high heels, fur coat and hat and gloves.

Rose began to cry. Phoebe ushered her into the house and sat her down and that was when Rose decided she would not tell anybody what had happened. She was too upset, too ashamed, and she did not want them to know that Jonas Ward owned her house. All she said was that she could no longer afford to stay there and must move, she didn't know what to do or where to go or what she would use for money.

'Oh dear, I'm so sorry,' Phoebe said. 'I'm sure you'll manage something. It cannot be that bad, you've always lived there. Mind you, I've always been glad we didn't have a great draughty house like that. They cost so much to keep up and if you did move to somewhere smaller I'm sure it would be better for you and Maddy. You could sell the place, then you'd have enough money to live well for years.'

She heard the outer door and got up.

'That'll be William. He's taking me into Newcastle. We're going out for lunch and to do some shopping. Maybe I could come up and see you tomorrow.'

She smiled as her husband came in.

'We have to leave and there is no money.'

'That cannot be right, Rose. Have you seen Edgar? You were meant to go and see him, weren't you?'

Evidently her friend was not listening.

'I've just been there, and he told me that I must leave.'

'Has the bank stepped in?' William said.

'Something like that.'

William nodded sagely.

'I knew it was only a matter of time,' he said. 'Come along, Phoebe, you'll miss the shops if we don't leave now.'

'I'll come and see you tomorrow,' Phoebe said, ushering her out. Rose had no alternative but to leave.

When they were sitting over the fire that night Rose told Maddy of her visit to the solicitor and of what had happened.

Maddy stared at her.

'This isn't our house any more?'

'No, it isn't.'

'But Daddy would never have sold it.'

'I think he thought he had no alternative.'

'So he sold it and didn't tell you?' Maddy said, and then realized that she was not making things any better, judging by the look on her mother's pale, thin face. When her mother said that they must move into the village, she did not understand.

'Where will we go?'

'I don't know.' Her mother's voice faltered.

Maddy was not used to that. The shock of having to leave the only home they had ever known, the place they had loved, was too much for them.

'This is our house. How could he sell it?'

'Your father knew that he was ill. We had no money.'

'Anything would have been better than losing the house,' Maddy cried.

'There's nothing we can do about it. We will have to move.'

'This house is our inheritance,' Maddy said. 'We can't leave here.'

'There is nothing else we can do. The man who owns it is insisting that we go.'

'Who is he?'

'He's called Jonas Ward. He's Edgar Ward's younger brother. A horrid man.'

'Is he going to come and live in the house?'

'I don't know what he's going to do with it. Perhaps he'll put tenants in. He doesn't live here and he's very rich apparently.'

'If he has so much money then why does he want to put us out?'

'I don't want to discuss this any more,' her mother said, almost in tears. 'We have to go, that's all there is to it. We will have to find somewhere else to live. And you must promise me that you will never tell anyone what I have just told you.'

'Is it a secret?'

'Yes. I will say to people only that we can no longer afford to live here. It's the truth.'

Maddy got up and hugged her mother.

'Don't worry,' she said, 'we'll find a little house somewhere and I'll get a job of some kind.'

She couldn't think what. There were few jobs in the village. The people who owned the shops worked in them themselves and she had no skills. Perhaps they would have to move away. That was a very frightening thought.

Maddy couldn't sleep when she went to bed. She didn't think her mother slept much either as she could hear her moving around the freezing bedroom. In the end Maddy got up and went next door to her and they got into bed and huddled together for warmth. The wind had got up and howled around the room.

Maddy could remember when she had been warm in bed with a fire and had been glad to hear the wind rushing around their house. She had been cosy in bed, safe with the sound of her parents talking in the bedroom next door. She knew she had only to call out for one of them and they would come to her. In the summer her bedroom door was left ajar so that she would not feel lonely but she never did in this house. She had always loved it so much.

On dark nights her mother would leave a lamp burning so there was never complete darkness and even in winter, when there were heavy curtains to keep out the draughts, Maddy loved to push back the curtains and see the moon and the stars, especially at this time of the year when it was frosty and the stars glinted through the night. It did not seem possible that they would have to go and leave it all.

Three

Rose waited. She waited several days for her friends to visit, for William Robson to offer her money to tide her over or for Bradley's friends like Gilbert Taylor, the biggest farmer in the district who owned several properties in the village, to come with their wives or at least for their wives to come to her and say that they understood, that they were sorry, that they would do everything they could to help. Rose was not especially friendly with Sophia Taylor, who thought she was a cut above everybody else, even though they were just farmers.

Nothing happened, nobody came until Rose began to doubt that Phoebe had understood, that perhaps she had told nobody. The only other explanation was that nobody cared, that nobody would assist her, and she could not and would not believe that. She had just over three weeks to leave. She determined to go down to the village the following day and see if any cottages were free.

If not then she and Maddy would have to leave the village and look elsewhere, and they would also have to find something to do which made money, though she could not think what. Her talent was homemaking and Maddy's money from the two old ladies would not even keep them in food. She would have to be brisk and practical and think of something soon.

Rose was not expecting Cuthbert Felix that morning. It was almost two weeks since the funeral and she still did not know what to do though she knew that she must do something. She had been into Sweet Wells and none of the cottages were free and although she asked around nobody knew of anything for rent. To her surprise Phoebe had told nobody of her problem as if she were embarrassed at her friend's difficulties or as though she did not believe Rose would really have to leave.

Rose had even travelled to Stanhope to look for a tiny house and something to do which would make money, but she had found nothing. She was desperate now.

She was not expecting anybody to call, had given up expecting any help, and she was planning to try again to find them somewhere to live now that she had grown used to the idea of losing the house for good. She was seated at her dining-room table thinking she must travel as far as Frosterley and even to Wolsingham.

Since her husband had been ill she had gradually been obliged to sell the animals so that they would have income. From a financial point of view he had been ill for a long time. Now she realized it was not something that would pass. Things would get worse.

The money from the sale of the few remaining animals would not keep them long and although people said that the Lord would provide she did not think he had been especially good at it so far. They must go from the house but to where? There must be a cottage of some kind that was free. Also she was beginning to be afraid that Jonas would wreak vengeance on them. She feared that one dark night men would come and throw out her furniture along with Maddy and herself and leave them out in the cold if she did not do something about her situation soon.

She must find work of some kind. She could not think what, but she would have to. Though Maddy was employed by the two old ladies to do their shopping, read to them, and keep the fires going, it did not make very much money.

The knocking on the front door was so unusual that she did not hear it at first. Everybody she knew came around to the side and up the yard into the back. She listened as it stopped, she waited and the person beyond the door waited, and then the knocking began again, louder. She got up, went through the hall, unlocked the door and drew it back.

The man who stood on the other side of it was fair, slight and around thirty. It was Cuthbert Felix. His family had always owned property in the village. He had until recently lived there with his mother, who had died last year. What he had done before or since Rose had no idea. No one knew him. He was well dressed, softly spoken, but did not join in anything in the village.

He had never gone to school and had had tutors at home. He had not been allowed to play with any of the other children. It made him strange but not objectionable somehow. He had a gentle manner and rather arresting brown eyes which contrasted well with his straight, floppy, straw-coloured hair, which gave him an air of delicacy, as though a strong wind would fell him. Every time she saw him Rose wanted to ask him whether he had eaten lunch that day.

He had not, that she remembered, been at Bradley's funeral with everybody else in the village, but if he had been at the back she might not have noticed him. It was possible that he could have been there and had been too shy to come up to the village hall afterwards.

'Mrs Grant, good morning.' He actually looked straight at her, something she could not remember him having ever done before.

She wished him good day and since he had no reason for coming here other than to visit her she invited him in. She offered to make tea but he declined, aware, no doubt, that she must abandon him for the kitchen.

Formalities over he did not seem to know what to say and paced about the room, wandering to the window and back and all around the floor, stopping each time he completed a circuit to view the morning. It was a lovely day now; sunshine spreading into the room and warming everything it touched. After he had completed two circuits he stopped in front of the black Frosterley Marble fireplace and regarded her narrowly.

He had a sweet gentle voice and Rose was surprised to find she was tempted to tell him everything that was amiss.

'Correct me if I am wrong, but I understand from village talk – you will forgive me – that you are obliged to leave your home.'

'That's right,' she said.

So people did know and no doubt they were talking about her circumstances. Rose was hurt to think that none of them cared sufficiently to come and see her and she couldn't think for a few seconds. She had to concentrate hard on what Mr Felix was saying and try not to think how odd that he had come all the way up here when nobody else had. She considered whether she had ever spoken to him before other than to wish him good day and then to wonder what on earth he was doing here.

'I own the grocery store in the village as no doubt you are aware. Mrs Maugham is getting too old to run it and is going to live with her married sister in Allendale. I wondered if you would be at all interested in taking it on.' He put up a hand as though she had begun to speak, which she had not. 'I don't need an answer immediately. You will naturally need time to think it over. Above the shop are living quarters. Nothing like you are used to, I know, but . . .'

Rose stared at him. She had a deliverer. She had given up hope that somebody might help and was resigned to having to find whatever she could, to do whatever she must. She could not believe it.

'It's very kind of you,' she said, completely taken aback and stammering over the one sentence she had uttered.

'Perhaps you would like to have a look round. You could send a note to my house with your daughter. Mrs Maugham will be moving within the next day or two. If you decide that it is not a good idea please just let me know. It probably isn't suitable at all for a lady such as yourself but it was all I could think of without giving offence and I just wanted to offer in case you were . . . at a loss as to what to do next.'

'Oh, Mr Felix, thank you so much. I am rather at a loss, as you must have guessed. How good of you to come all this way to try to help.'

'Not at all.' He seemed embarrassed. Did his cheeks glow or was it just the brightness of the winter sunshine?

Rose could have kissed him and was so grateful she had

to be careful to keep her composure. She wanted to cry too and since she could do neither she kept her face stiff and observed the decencies.

She thanked him again and when she had seen him to the door she thought how strange it was that the only offer of help she had had was from someone she barely knew. As she closed the door the thought came back to her. God will provide.

The opportunity had arisen. It was the only one so far. She must not hope for more. She could not afford to wait.

Cuthbert went home. He dreaded the darkness and the long night ahead. He walked as slowly as he could across the village square and up to the big iron gates which led to the drive leading to his house. It was the biggest house in the village. That had mattered to his mother. It was stone with big pillars in front of the door, nothing modest about it, but then she had wanted the place to be impressive.

She had enjoyed being the richest and most important person in the village though Cuthbert had thought his mother lonely, being too high and mighty to speak to anyone other than to speak down to the shopkeepers. His father had made a lot of money at something, but it was never spoken of. His mother spoke of his father with reverence as a gentleman, but he must have made his money at something, it stood to reason, Cuthbert thought. He had a feeling it was railways. He didn't remember his father very well.

His mother had always talked about Hexham House being the biggest house in the village. She came from Hexham and was very proud of the fact. Hexham being full of cultured people according to his mother. Perhaps they would have been better to move there after his father died, but she liked being what was called a big fish in a little pond.

She had renamed the house when she began living there and was proud that it was bigger than the doctor's; though not prettier Cuthbert had always wanted to say. Mrs Robson was a keen gardener and even in the winter there was colour. He admired that. Nothing seemed to grow in his garden; he killed off what he planted. He was so clumsy, so inept.

It was bigger than the Taylors' house she thought, and unlike it in that it had some form of garden around it whereas theirs was rather cluttered by barns and byres and tractors and the workers' cottages. It could not be said to be neat; it was too busy for that.

He envied the busyness of it because he did not know how to be busy. Mr Taylor was always going to marts and meeting other farmers, and he shot in the autumn and helped to organize the local agricultural shows. His wife was on various committees and they had help in the house, and she wore hats with feathers, rings outside of her long gloves and always wore lipstick.

Hexham House was bigger than Mr Ward's house, though Cuthbert could not help thinking Mr Ward had no pretensions whatsoever. Mr Ward had no claims to anything in the village. His wife had gone, nobody knew where, and everybody knew there was always a good reason for these things.

There had been a whisper some time ago when Cuthbert was quite young that Edgar Ward had killed his wife and buried her somewhere up on the fells, but Cuthbert thought this was most unlikely. Mr Ward was what you called 'prosaic', too much the solicitor to do anything as exciting or awful.

He was the kind of person people relied on to get matters right so what had gone on between him and his wife nobody knew and these days few people cared. He was not eligible like a widower. He was just there.

His house, though large, was on the end of the street and not being a detached house had no importance of any kind. Also Mr Ward was noted for being very careful with his money and was unpopular the odd time he went to anything social because he would never pay for anything.

Not that Cuthbert cared about how large his house was. He never had cared and had only cared that his mother should be content and she had been. Their house in fact was the only house which had a claim to be as big as Grant House, the place high up on the fell tops where, he thought with a little shudder, people said ghosts walked from centuries ago. There were tales of the Border Reivers coming over the tops and stealing sheep and women, and slaughtering men.

Mrs Grant would be well away from that place and if she had to go and work in his shop then so be it. He hated that all he could offer her was the shop. He wished so much that he could have done more. The house was so far out that he worried about Rose Grant and her child up there by themselves. Cuthbert felt that anything could happen and nobody would be any the wiser.

He let himself into his house. The fire was on. Bessie Everton and Lil Meikle from Stanhope were his help and they came daily to clean and cook and lay the fires. The place smelled of beeswax. His mother had been particular about these things and since she had been dead only a year he felt as though he must keep up her standards.

There were flowers in big vases in the hall. It occurred to him for the first time that he didn't need to do that. He didn't care about flowers and it made him feel better that he could make a change and his mother would not be there to contradict him or complain. It made him feel much more powerful than ever before. If he could change small things like that he might go on to make other bigger changes in time.

He sat down in front of his fire with his slippers and his smoking jacket on, with a glass of port beside him sitting next to a cigar. He thought of what it had been like when his mother would not let him smoke or drink or bring anybody to the house. Taking an evening drink was a change he had made as soon as she died, but he had told himself it was grief whereas in fact he now acknowledged that it was indulgence.

His tutors had never stayed long, they had never been good enough for his mother, but he had learned quite a lot of things, all of them useless: several languages, mathematics, geography. He had liked geography and had made plans. He had really thought that after his mother died he might take the opportunity, but somehow, coming back to the house alone and realizing he now had no one, it seemed pointless to go anywhere. Surely when travelling you needed somebody there to point out places to and appreciate views and food with.

You needed somebody to talk to, to enjoy it, and he had no one. He had never made any friends as his mother would not let him play football on the green with the other boys, and he remembered watching longingly at them playing while he was kept inside on the long summer evenings when it barely got dark before twelve.

He found that he did not know what to say to people now. He had felt as though he had had to speak to Mrs Grant – he had not known what to say to her and he wished very much to help her. There was something about the turn of her shoulders and her distressed eyes which unsettled him.

She was older than him, but it didn't feel like that to him. He felt the same age as Rose Grant, as though he had lived a long time already. He was so glad that he had been able to help her. She had barely been able to restrain her gratitude, and it made him warm to think that she could still live in the village and it had been made possible by him.

He must be certain not to go into the shop too often. He didn't want her to think he was going to get in her way or give her too much advice about what to do. Mrs Grant was an intelligent woman, she would manage. He would just be there to help as much as he could when she needed anyone. If he did too much people would talk and that would never do.

Four

The grocery shop in Sweet Wells was one of the least interesting places Maddy had seen and she could not believe they might be going to live there. From the moment they stepped inside she wanted to run back up the hill to their house.

She thought that Mr Felix was strange. He wasn't married in the first place and that was almost unheard of. All the men in the village were married except for men who were very old and were widowed but you didn't get many of those. Mr Ward, the solicitor was on his own, but Maddy had heard that he'd once had a wife who had died when Sep had been a little boy.

She and Sep had been in the same class at school when they were little, before he had been sent away to school. She had liked him but since then she had hardly seen him. His father did not go to church so nobody saw him except when they needed legal things sorting out and Sep virtually disappeared.

The shop took up the whole of the ground floor. Behind it was a big room for storing goods and then a backyard with big gates and beyond it the unmade back lane, full of potholes which held big puddles when it rained.

A narrow staircase led to the living quarters. Up them there were two bedrooms, a living room and a kitchen and none of them was big. The whole lot would have gone into the sitting room at home. It was clean though, it even smelled clean, and that was all you could say for it really, Maddy thought.

Mrs Maugham, who ran the shop, said very little but she looked relieved. Maybe when you were that old running a shop was nothing but a bother and she was keen to move out. She said as much. She was very chatty. Maddy supposed that came from dealing with people all day so she felt obliged to make conversation. Mrs Maugham was leaving straight away, going to live with her sister and glad she was to get away. She told Maddy that her old bones wouldn't take the stairs any more and shifting stuff about and on and off the shelves needed a younger person. Folk were so demanding these days, she said, nothing was ever enough. You were expected to be at their beck and call all the time.

Her mother told Mr Felix straight away that they would take the place. Maddy wished she wouldn't. She wished there was something else they could do, some way they could stay in their house. She couldn't believe they were going to end up in the shop, putting up with the boys fighting outside over sherbet dips and serving cough drops to old ladies.

They would have to cut up slabs of butter, wrap it in greaseproof paper, and put up with having the farmers coming in trailing cow muck on their wellingtons and having to serve people who had been their friends with things like flour and sugar and lard.

Her mother went to visit Thomas Allen who owned the auction rooms in Stanhope. Maddy waited outside until her fingers and toes were frozen. Then she and her mother trudged back up the hill. It was bitterly cold and Maddy was glad when they reached the house.

It would be one of the last times they did so, she thought. How odd to live in the village. The noises would be quite different. She tried to think positively about the move but couldn't. There was not one single thing she could think of which would be better.

Their supper was very late and all the light had gone before they sat down to it. They would have Christmas without her father. She didn't see how they would bear it. Why did it have to be Christmas soon, the time of year which people always spent with their families?

As she did the washing-up, her mother disappeared upstairs and when Maddy ventured up there later she found her mother was packing most of her father's clothes. Rose wanted to keep one or two items, Maddy could see, though she had said nothing. Maybe it was just from sentiment.

'I promised Mrs Philips these. Some poor soul will be glad of them,' her mother said.

'Our furniture isn't going to fit,' Maddy said.

'I've asked Thomas Allen to take most of our furniture to the auction rooms on Tuesday and he'll send somebody for the rest of our goods on Wednesday so we'll be sleeping in the village by Wednesday night. We'll take the beds and the dining furniture and sufficient easy chairs as long as they will fit in—'

'And the books?'

'The books won't fit. I'm sorry,' her mother said. 'We have to stick to essentials, clothing and kitchenware and crockery, cutlery and the like, cooking pots and such. The old writing desk will have to go, I'm afraid.'

The writing desk, oak, Edwardian, ornate, had been their father's favourite piece of furniture.

'Won't we need it for doing the accounts?' Maddy asked.

'We can do those on the kitchen table,' she replied with more briskness than Maddy thought she felt. 'We can sell it. God knows we need the money.'

'What about the piano?' Maddy didn't want to talk about it; she couldn't bear to think of anybody else having it.

Her mother didn't look at her.

'Mr Allen says it isn't worth enough to take the trouble of hauling it all the way down the hill, it won't make enough money,' she said.

Firstly her mother had lost her husband, now she was losing her house and her child's home and inheritance. It worried Maddy so much and she felt as though nothing was safe any more. Who could lose their home? Yet she knew that it happened to people all the time, but it just seemed so unbelievable.

She tried to be like her mother and get on being busy but it was difficult. There was one question that she dared not ask and in the end she did not have to. The day they had to leave their house her mother came to her and her face was dark. She tried to speak and couldn't. They stood in the darkness of the sitting room. It was early morning. What little sun there was had not yet ventured into any part of the house.

'We can't take the piano either,' she said.

Her mother's words fell from her mouth like the stones had fallen on to the road once up past Alston when she had been a very little girl, tumbling and breaking as though she had been rehearsing, as though she would have done anything rather than let them be uttered. Maddy gazed across to the instrument.

'There's nowhere to put it,' her mother went on quickly. 'The downstairs is taken up with the shop and the stairs are steep and narrow and go round. I'm sorry, Maddy, I know it's important to you, but we cannot.'

'Maybe we could sell it,' Maddy said brightly because she was numb and nothing mattered now. And she knew very well that the only thing which did matter, the only thing which possibly ever mattered, was money.

'I don't see how we would ever get it down the hill without a great deal of bother and it is very old. If Mr Allen doesn't think it's worth anything then who would want it?' her mother said.

The piano had been such an important part of her childhood. Long before she had gone to school – and often in the winter she didn't go at all because the weather was too bad – her mother had taught her to read and write and add up and her father would read stories to her on long summer afternoons in the garden or take her for walks and name flowers, trees and birds so she now remembered the names of them all. She had helped her mother to make cakes, scones and bread. She'd loved the smell of the warm kitchen and would go into the village to buy flour, sugar and cherries and big slabs of creamy yellow butter.

When she had been very small she had liked going to various people's houses and would sit, listening to the conversation, though really distracted by other sights and sounds so that what people were saying would fade into the background as she watched the sunlight fall on raindrops and the way the leaves fluttered in a slight breeze, the fading colours in the autumn or the way a tabby cat moved slowly across the lawn in search of prey.

Her greatest joy had always been the piano. It had been her grandmother's. She had been the last person to play it before Maddy. Her own mother claimed she had no talent. For a long time when Maddy had been very small it sat alone in the corner of the room against the wall.

It was an upright piano, a dear looking thing in dark wood with shiny gold bits inside the wood like an extra flourish for decoration. There were holders for candlesticks at either side though they had never, as far as she could remember, held candles. She did not think she could remember her grandmother playing though her mother said her grandmother had been skilled, but she had been ill since before Maddy was born and had never left the little hill farm which Rose's parents owned.

She felt sure that if she had wanted her parents would have paid for lessons but her playing the piano was not like that. One afternoon when she was seven her mother and father were in the kitchen and she went over and after listening for the sound of their footsteps in the hall she lifted the lid and regarded the black and white keys with awe. She loved reading, the look of letters on pages and how they were made up into stories and information, but the little groups of black and white keys seemed readable too.

She stood listening to her heartbeat and the sound of her parents' voices. Were they getting nearer? She decided they were not. No footsteps invaded the hall. She waited, holding her breath, determined to slam down the lid, but she went on holding it until finally she pushed it back until it rested against the piano and stayed there by itself. Then she sat down on the velvet-topped stool and let her fingers touch the keys.

They were cold. The room was only heated during the evenings even though this was October. The cool autumn wind moved the grass in the fields outside, she could see it from the corners of her eyes as she tried first to look at the piano and then not to.

Her hands on the keys felt to her like reaching the comfort

and safety of home after the day had been frightening, like the time she had met a tramp in the village who had called out to her and begged her for money when her mother was further along the street, talking to a friend, or when she had skipped ahead and lost her mother for what had seemed like a long time.

It was as if the music knew her. When she moved her fingers the notes came out and not only made delicate sounds, but they came out in a pattern. She had not known they were going to. The patterns somehow came from the piano to her and back again and as she played she recognized the tune. It was one of her mother's favourite hymns – 'Now Thank We All Our God'.

Halfway into the second verse, mentally singing the words, she realized that her mother and father were both in the room and she stopped. Her mother was smiling, her father was smiling too and telling her how clever she was.

It was her favourite memory, discovering she could play – she never had had lessons, it was never like that, just something instinctive and fun to do – and when she thought of him now he was for ever standing there in the pale autumn afternoon sunlight.

They moved. Maddy tried to keep in her memory the life she had had together up on the tops with her parents. It was not perfect of course. Her father had been ill for so long that she could not remember the last time he had worked so money had always been a problem and what money they had had dwindled over the years so that now they had nothing but the pennies she made. At least her mother had spared her father the grocery store, the cramped rooms and strangeness. And she had spared him the leaving of their house on the tops which would soon be gone for ever for her.

When the last of what they were taking was gone, when they walked away, following their furniture and belongings down the long narrow winding road which led into the village, when the views around their land were all up in the distance, only then could Maddy bear the idea that she would not live there any more.

The little house above the shop was so cramped. Her window looked out across the square and there were icicles outside her window. There had been snow earlier that morning.

She watched the children sliding on the ice. They had spent a long time creating a slide on the first day and now because it was Saturday they were standing in a queue and taking turns. They seemed to enjoy it. Even when they stumbled, slipped, lost their balance and fell, very often on their bottoms, all they did was laugh. She envied them being small and having only the present to think of.

She had not known how often she would think about the piano. At first she thought of it and her father and the house fondly and that she would be able to bear her life as it was; in the few shabby rooms with the noise of the shop below, her mother greeting people with her soft, polite voice, the tinkle of the bell as they came in, the sounds of a transaction taking place.

She liked it best when they were going, when they left, when the quietness followed. It did not last, always there was somebody coming into the shop. Maddy knew that was important, that her mother needed the custom in order to make a living, to make money, their very survival depended upon it, but Maddy still liked it best when it was late, when the shop was quiet, and her mother came upstairs to make the tea.

Maddy thought they managed very well. She thought she was going to be all right until one cold, dark night when she woke up with a fleeting dream, pushing away from her so that all she remembered was its essence: that her father was calling her.

She opened her eyes. She lay there for a few moments and then, as her eyes discerned dark and lighter shadows and the furniture in the corners, she lay still for a few more seconds. Then she got up and pulled on her clothes which were folded neatly on the chair beside her bed. She crept down the stairs, taking coat, gloves, scarf and boots with her and, sliding the bolts in the back door, she let herself out into the yard.

Various empty crates were stacked neatly there. She went to the gates, drew back the bolts in this as well, and stepped out into the night, surprised at how light it was with a big full moon and a sky full of stars.

She had rarely been out at night. It was the ideal time for her, she decided. Nobody was about, not a single person roamed the village streets. She was not afraid, that was the other strange thing, she did not think about being afraid and was joyful and light instead.

She did not even have to decide what she was going to do. For many days she had pictured the house and the piano and she began to trudge up the cold snowy slope. She did not look back. Even when an owl swooped low around her she was not bothered at all. She had always thought they were the creatures most like her: shy, hiding in corners, coming out when nobody could see them. The owl was friendly. She saw the dark of its wings, like a visitor who had only stopped to say hello and then it was gone and she was walking up towards the house.

She was pleased now, excited and it did not seem to take long for her to reach the building. She had thought it would look different but it didn't. The windows were boarded up, her mother had told her that and she did not even try the doors. She only wondered at the man who owned it not wanting to be here. Perhaps he had never seen it so he would not know how beautiful it was.

She went straight round to the side door, down the narrow path and there she could see the little window which was just above the sink and she knew that even though other people might think it locked people who had lived there for years knew very well that all you had to do was pull at the bottom of it and it would gradually come open.

She had always let herself in like that if her mother was out when she came home when she was younger. It gave as she pulled and then she had to go and get the little stool which lived behind the hedge and place it carefully underneath to allow her to ease herself in.

It had become more difficult to do as she grew older and got bigger, but she was not a large girl or a fat one. I can't get any fatter either or I won't fit, she thought. She could only just squeeze in. Nobody of any size would have done it.

She got down from the wooden board beside the sink on to the floor and stood, listening and watching. The doors were closed but none of the downstairs rooms were locked so she opened the door, went into the hall and straight into the sitting room and there was the piano, standing in a pool of light which fell in from the moon shining beyond the window.

She sat down on the piano stool and lifted the lid and instantly began to play and she could feel happiness coursing through her as the sound of the patterns of the notes she was making filled the room and the whole house.

She did not fear her father's ghost. She could feel the presence of the past and how happy they had been there until he was taken ill. She played for him, all his favourite tunes, all the songs he had so much liked and she could feel how pleased he was, how he had waited for her to come back so that she would play for him this one last time.

Five

'You'll have to be careful,' Phoebe Robson said.

'What do you mean?' Rose said.

The two women looked at each other across the short distance of the easy chairs in the sitting room.

'Cuthbert Felix is very odd and there were a good many people would have liked to run the shop. You're old enough to be his mother.'

Rose laughed. It was the first time she had laughed in ages though somehow she felt besmirched by their insinuations and sorry for Cuthbert Felix. He was the only person who had offered her help, though they seemed not to notice this, as though the move had happened automatically.

'He's just a boy,' she said, 'and it was very kind of him. Besides, who could need the shop more than I do?'

Phoebe looked puzzled and Rose could not help thinking with a sigh that she knew nothing about money, she was a married woman, she didn't need to. Her husband was a very important man in the dale being the local doctor.

'He's a very strange young man,' Phoebe said.

'Some people lead more difficult lives than others,' Rose said.

Phoebe was wearing a lovely expensive frock made from blue silk and when she had taken off her gloves her hands and nails were perfect.

Rose regarded her broken nails, her hands red from the moving, housework and rearranging, and then she heard the sound of Maddy singing downstairs as she stacked tins on to the shelves and thought things were not so bad.

Phoebe started chatting about the dinner dance she was going to at the weekend. She had bought a new dress in

Fenwicks' French Salon, the department store in Newcastle. It was black and green silk, full-length. Rose knew what it would be like, long and flowing with a train, and Phoebe would be wearing high heels and gloves to her elbows. She would be wearing the silver bangle which Will had given her for her birthday last month.

They would be going to one of the big hotels in the area and they would drink Martini cocktails and chat and there would be a band and they would waltz and Phoebe's dress would swing in time to the music and her husband would be wearing evening dress, black with a white shirt and black bow-tie, and it would be so glamorous.

She could remember the last time she and Bradley had gone with them, before he was ill. It felt like such a long time ago and she had been as light-hearted then as Phoebe was now. She and Bradley would stay at the hotel often because it was so far to get home while some friend from the village stayed at their house and looked after Maddy, and she would return the next day, tired from enjoying herself.

She did not like hearing what a good time they would be having while she was upstairs alone in the little shop with nothing to do and nobody to go dancing with. But then, she thought, it would have been worse if Phoebe had not thought she could speak freely in front of her. She thought of her friend complaining amiably about her husband and wishing she had a husband who would stay too late at the surgery.

When the tea had been drunk and Phoebe had gone, Rose looked around her new house and shuddered. What if Felix Cuthbert was somehow difficult or odd or made a nuisance of himself now that she had the shop? She tried to remember if he had taken special notice of her daughter, concerned he had a motive, and decided not, but it was all so worrying. She carried her heavy heart back up the stairs.

Six

Tick-tock. Tick-tock. The bloody clock, Septimus Ward thought. He should have put that clock through the window. It sat on the dining-room sideboard. It had always sat there and throughout the meal it made that noise until people felt obliged to compete with it, saying stupid things rather than leaving the clock booming into the silence.

It had been his grandmother's and must have pride of place as though time was the most important thing of all and the worst about that was that it was true. Did people have to have something so beautiful, so ornate, so shiny, inlaid with a darker wood, all intricate and curly so that the clockmaker could show off his incredible ability? Did he not know that he was measuring out people's lives?

When he had been a little boy Sep had not wanted to go away to school, but his parents had insisted. You couldn't tell people you didn't want to leave your mother. How stupid that would sound, how babyish and though it was true he could barely acknowledge it to himself.

It was not far away, his mother said, the few miles into Durham City. Sep wanted to suggest that he could go as a day boy and come home every evening, but he couldn't and his parents didn't suggest it. He felt like he was going to the ends of the earth.

He couldn't complain. His father must be obeyed, and if you didn't obey he had a tendency to catch you across the face so finely that it stung for hours and there was never any point in complaining about anything because no matter how afraid he might be he was always more afraid of his father. Maybe all fathers were like that, he had never dared ask anybody if theirs were any different to his.

He remembered going home at the end of the school year for the summer holidays for the first time. He had so much looked forward to it. So he was rather surprised to reach home, run out of the car and into the house, shouting his mother's name to no reply. He ran upstairs and then back down and his father was standing in the hall, not looking at him and not saying anything, and even from there he could hear the blasted dining-room clock. Its sound seemed to echo through the hall.

Mrs Herries, who did the cooking, came out of the kitchen and fussed and then went back in again, looking red in the face and wet around the eyes. Sep thought that it was just because she was baking and it was hot in the kitchen. He could smell lovely little cakes, jam tarts with soft yellow spongy tops. It was one of the best smells in the world. He hoped she would offer him cakes for tea.

'I was trying to tell you . . .' his father said and then stopped.

Sep didn't understand. He hadn't heard his father trying to tell him anything. In fact his father had done nothing but put his trunk into the back of the car and greet him as usual without affection.

All he said was, 'Have you had a good term?' because they had not seen one another since Easter. There had been some confusion, something about his parents going away and he had stayed in Durham with one of the day boys, Harrison, who was all right but other people's homes were never like your own. He had missed his parents, especially his mother.

There was something wrong. He had known all through the term somehow that there was, but you couldn't do anything about it with grown-ups because they didn't tell you anything. He couldn't ask anything either and had missed his mother a lot more than he would have admitted to anyone.

'Where is she?' he ventured.

'She's gone.' His father still didn't look at him.

She was dead, that was it, she had died. He had known there was something the matter because at Christmas she was so quiet, and at Easter she was so thin and his father looked downright awful now and he knew what it was, that she must never be mentioned any more because she had gone to God, was in heaven.

'You didn't tell me,' he accused softly.

'I didn't know how to,' his father said.

Sep thought that wasn't fair. Adults were supposed to know how to say things to small boys when their mothers died. Nobody at school had told him though he would not have been able to go to the funeral, somehow you weren't allowed to as though you would miss people less because you hadn't been told and hadn't been invited.

He didn't even cry. His eyes stung. He had already learned at school that you couldn't because only babies cried. And it seemed to him that everybody at home was used to the idea, that they had known for so long that it didn't matter, and his feelings didn't matter.

Nobody said they were sorry, nobody cared. The best Mrs Herries could do was enquire as to what time Mr Ward wanted supper. Sep didn't even bother to run outside. Nobody would have come after him and he couldn't eat the little cakes which he had thought he wanted so much.

It was a long time until supper, the longest day of his life. There were great big holes where his mother would have been, in the sitting room and in the garden which she loved so much. There were no flowers in the house as she had always arranged them. There were no plants any more in the conservatory. It was empty and smelled of dead roses.

He went to bed without her kiss as he had done for so long. In a way it was easier to pretend he was at school so that he would not expect it. His father would not have kissed him goodnight, his father did not even see him to bed. He was too old for that. Sep would stop at the study door to say goodnight and his father would not even look up from his desk.

Night after night that summer, with the windows open so he could hear the sheep bleating in the fields and cars making their way down the narrow winding dales road towards Durham, he lay there thinking about his mother and the awful distance between them and what it must be like to die and leave everybody behind you.

Things had been like that until the autumn term of this year and then he had seen her walking on the towpath by the river just below the school. It was one of the strangest experiences of his life.

He had gone down there to smoke. He needn't have bothered. They were on the verge of kicking him out anyway because he had broken so many rules, given up going to classes completely, had long since stopped doing sport or joining in. He was standing by the river, it was the most famous view in Durham City, right opposite to the cathedral and the old fulling mill, next to the mill on this bank where the weir was and big birds like herons perched to grab at the fish that came by, and there was his mother, walking towards him, talking and laughing, just as she had been when he was a small boy.

He stopped and stared and then didn't know what to do. She was going to come right past him. In confusion he turned away as though the bitterly cold breeze was spoiling his efforts at trying to keep a match alight and he stayed that way until she had gone past, and then he turned around and watched.

It had been wet for the past few weeks and the towpath was muddy. Autumn had taken its hold on the leaves, the few that were left on the trees were bare and black, the river was heavy with water, white flecked above the grey and the towpath was a blanket of leaves: soggy, dark and ragged.

The two women went immediately out of sight, going around the mill on its narrow path, hidden by the building. Sep panicked, thinking he might lose sight of them altogether. They could go across the old stone bridge just up from there, Prebends, which led up to the bailey and on to the cathedral and the town, they might go back up towards the school or further on past the bridge and even if they chose to go over it there were three different ways.

He threw the cigarette on the ground, put his foot on it and went after them. They strolled into the middle of the bridge and stood there. He stayed to one side and watched. His instincts told him to let her go, but he couldn't. He hadn't seen her in ten years.

He waited. After a very long time the women went on, chatting, to the side of the bridge and then began to walk up the cobbles of the bailey at the bottom end of the cathedral and down the narrow path which led to Saddler Street, past the shops and into the market place and up Claypath which led up a steep bank and out in a northerly direction away from the city. Halfway up the bank they went into a house with a blue door.

He banged on the door and when it was opened he pushed past the woman who had been with his mother. She shouted after him. The hall was painted dark brown and in the sitting room a small fire burned and a square-paned window looked out across the city. His mother was standing in front of the fire.

'Glynis!' the other declared, 'this boy forced his way inside.'

His mother looked across at him.

'We have nothing of any worth,' she said.

So much for uniform was all he could think. An expensive public school wasn't doing anything for him here. They thought he was a thief, an intruder. She didn't even recognize him, he thought bitterly.

She was so pretty, just as he remembered. His own dark eyes looked back at him. Her hair was black like his. She had been born on a remote Scottish island he could never remember the name of. She was slight and had high cheekbones and curving red lips and glossy white teeth. He remembered her goodnight kisses on the forehead and how, when he had been very small, she would sing him to sleep with wonderful lilting Scottish songs.

She went on looking at him. He went on letting her.

'Good heavens,' she said, as they stared at one another. 'How you've grown.'

Yes, he thought savagely, I'm bigger than I was ten years ago.

'Who is this?' the other woman asked.

'This is my son, Septimus.'

She had landed him with a bloody name like that and then had walked out and left him.

'My, my!' The other woman walked around him like he was an exhibit in a museum.

He wanted to say stupid obvious things and was afraid he might begin to cry, something he hadn't done in years but knew he was too angry for that.

'What are you doing here?' his mother asked.

'What am I doing here? I go to school here. Don't you remember?'

She looked away, gazing into the fire. Finally, he thought, she was ashamed.

'Yes,' she said, 'I remember.'

'How long have you lived in Durham?'

She hesitated for a few seconds and when she spoke her voice trembled.

'Always,' she said.

Sep couldn't believe it. Now he really wanted to cry.

'Your father and I . . . we thought it best that you didn't see me.'

'And why was that best?'

She didn't answer. He gave her lots of time and then he repeated the question. Her thin fingers twisted themselves around one another and he tried not to think how she used to cuddle him to her when he was scared of the dark, when he was very small. He wished he could be that small again so that she would take him into her arms just once more.

He tried to remember what it was like, what she smelled of, what she felt like and savour her kisses on his temple. He had felt like her love was the best he would ever have and it had gone. He was not good enough, he did not matter.

'Why—?' he began again, and the other woman said, 'Because of me.'

Sep turned on her. He had thought she might at least have had sufficient tact to leave them alone. He didn't like her, he had already decided. He had known the moment he saw her that he wouldn't like her and it was a feeling full of male prejudice, even he knew that.

She looked like a man dressed as a woman or the other way round. She was short, fat, had two chins and wore trousers and a shirt. She was repulsive to him. Large breasts strained beneath her shirt, a fat stomach protruded below the waistband and spilled above it. He was only glad he couldn't see her arse. She had fat thighs.

And just in case he was stupid, she said, 'Your mother left your father for me.'

He was terribly inclined to laugh. How could his mother have left his father for this dumpling? If she had been physically beautiful . . . if she had even had graceful hands, a lovely speaking voice or any obvious intelligence somehow it would have helped. His mother had left his father for a gnome.

And then he thought, no, surely his mother had run away because his father was a bully. But he had been a small boy and she had left him. He had been her child. Was that less important?

Apparently it was. She had run to somebody who so obviously cared for her. He remembered how their steps had matched when they walked past him, how they stood on the bridge and talked and smiled. His mother was safe and happy with this woman. Who could ask for more than that?

He left. He couldn't stand any more. He ran from the house and away back down the steep hill and into the town.

He couldn't rest. He couldn't think about anything else. He tried to sleep, but he lay there imagining her opening the blue door to him. Her face would light up when she saw him and she would ask him in.

The other woman was conveniently not there and not allowed into this fantasy of perfection. It was Christmas and the fire was lit. His mother sat him down in front of it with a toasting fork. He realized he was going back into his early childhood because on winter Sunday afternoons he and his mother had often sat over the fire when the light faded and they had toasted crumpets for tea.

This sweet imagining lasted him through three days and then he began to long for the sight of her. He walked through the town and hung about in Claypath one evening until it was late, until the light had been gone for hours, hoping for a glimpse of her.

Thinking she might walk past him as she had done before, or down the bank and into the house he waited. He stood there waiting for the lights to come on but nothing happened. The house remained in darkness. Where could she be? What did people do in cities on cold autumn nights? Go to the theatre, visit friends, have supper? He was jealous of whoever she was with.

He went back to school, hoping during the days that followed that he would see her along the towpath or on the narrow pavements along the cobbled street or going across Elvet Bridge into town or on Palace Green in front of the cathedral, but he did not.

Every day he was convinced that he saw her disappearing around corners or into shops, but it was never her and after another fruitless week he knocked on the house next door in the late afternoon and enquired as to whether they knew if the two ladies were at home.

A short, stocky man said, 'Oh, no, they've gone.'

Sep stared into the light of the house behind him. The street had suddenly become such a friendless place that he was not sure he could stand it any longer and would surely burst past the man who guarded his own doorway and run through into the sitting room in the stupid and mistaken belief that his mother had popped in there to visit as neighbours did.

'Gone? What, gone on holiday or visiting?'

'No, gone for good. A moonlight flit apparently. Left everything. Didn't even pay their rent,' the man said, and he went in and closed the door.

She had run away again, Sep thought and this time it was not from his father. She had run away from him.

Seven

On Christmas morning Maddy found it impossible to sing carols with her father not there, especially when they got to 'Hark the Herald Angels Sing' because that had been his favourite. He always sang very loudly and when she had been a little girl she had been embarrassed, but the last few years she had enjoyed listening to him because he had a nice voice, a good voice, in tune. Now it was silenced for ever.

Afterwards everybody stood around, talking on the porch. She wandered away to her father's grave, thinking about how awful it must be for him not to be there to share their Christmas dinner.

They didn't have any money, she knew, but her mother had bought a turkey – actually she hadn't bought it, she had swapped Mr Bell, who kept the best turkeys in the area, a big box of groceries for it, and the good thing about running the grocery store was that at least you had plenty to eat at Christmas.

There had been no presents, just nuts and fruit in her Christmas stocking. She was not a child any more, she shouldn't mind, but somehow she did. She was standing there thinking about the lavish Christmases they had had when she was small and she promised herself she would go for a walk up to the house that afternoon, just to see how it did without her.

Her mother was becoming more and more tired. Maddy did not want to leave her, but she fell asleep on the sofa so Maddy left her a little note and went out because the afternoon was fine and it would not last long. She walked up the fields. It had snowed several days earlier though not, to other people's disappointment, today, but it had been cold and there was enough snow to make it Christmassy. The farmers were out scattering hay for the sheep, which gathered as soon as they saw the men coming towards them. They did not get a day off for Christmas. The sheepdog which belonged to Mr Walton was with him in the field as she went by. She waved and he waved back and let the dog go. It came over to her, wagging its tail. She got down and talked to it and hugged it before Mr Walton whistled and it scuttled away at a great pace.

There was nobody anywhere near the house, but she could see before she got there that the front door, which had been boarded up, along with the windows, was not boarded up any longer. Some of the downstairs windows had had the wood wrenched from their windows too.

She opened the door and stepped inside, wondering whether vagrants were living there. A lot of men had come back from the Great War and taken to the road since there were no jobs for them and it would have been silly not to have taken advantage of an opportunity such as an empty house in such weather. Although it was a long way out from the village people did walk along the top road very often.

She felt like an intruder which was ridiculous in her own home. The owner had not come here and he had obviously sent people to board it up so she should not feel like that, but if there were unknown men in the house then perhaps it was foolish to go in.

She stopped in the hall. There was no sound of any kind except . . . yes, the crackling of logs. Somebody was there. She almost turned and ran out and her mother would have been horrified that she did not. She trod silently along the hall. It was strange to her because so much of their furniture had been left. In some ways it was as if they had just stepped out. It had been impractical to move it; none of it had any worth otherwise her mother would have sold it.

Old chairs, old tables, old sofas and her piano were of no value to anyone and her mother would have had to pay to get them brought down the hill. So in some ways it was as though she and her father and mother had just stepped out or gone away for a few days except that the house was freezing as never before.

The sitting-room door was not shut, though it was pushed to as though somebody had meant to keep the draught from the hall at bay. She pushed it open, making very little sound. It was light. She had to stop herself from exclaiming out loud.

The brightness of the snow and the great flames from the fire combined to ensure it was as welcoming as it had ever been and the huge old sofa which would have not fitted into their new home, or anybody else's because it was so torn and shabby, was occupied. A tall, lean, dark-haired boy was asleep there. She soon saw why. There was a bottle of whisky on the floor, half-empty. What kind of boy did such a thing?

At first she hesitated, thinking it was a party of some kind and that he had friends with him who were obviously not nice people. A pack of cigarettes was there too and an ornate slim silver lighter.

As she got closer she recognized him. It was Sep Ward, Edgar Ward's son and only child. Maddy let go of her breath. Sep would not hurt her, at least she didn't think so. She didn't know him very well as he had been away for years at school and rarely come back in the holidays. It seemed a strange thing to her, his father had lived in Sweet Wells since his mother had died when they were very small, but somehow Sep had never been there. What was he doing here now?

He opened his eyes on cue. They were black and heavily lashed and Maddy stopped. Her instant reaction was that he didn't look anything like Mr Ward, his mother had been Scottish and he was dark like she imagined people from the Western Islands might be. She didn't know why. He sat up, looking around him vaguely as people did when they had slept.

'What are you doing here?' he said.

Maddy was indignant.

'Me? I live here, at least I used to. Was it you who took the boards from the door and the windows?'

'It looked so gloomy,' he said. 'Sorry about your dad.'

He was the first person who had said that to her, usually people said it to her mother as though the loss had been only her mother's. Children, even those her age, were not considered to have lost anything, they were not even allowed at funerals, but she had insisted on going. She knew one or two people had looked askance, but she didn't care. He had been her father and she had wanted to say goodbye, as though you ever say goodbye, she thought now, plumping down in the chair nearest the fire.

'You've got a good blaze going,' she said.

He grinned.

'The boards from the door and windows,' he said.

'Nice,' Maddy said, and she felt a wave of happiness. How ridiculous to be so pleased just because he had made the house look hospitable.

'Want a drink?'

She eyed the bottle.

'Go on,' he said.

She didn't like to say yes because she didn't know anything about drinking, but she didn't want to say no because in some ridiculous way it seemed like she was spoiling the part.

'I'm not drinking out the bottle,' she said, and she went off to the kitchen and found glasses in one of the cupboards. They were rather dusty, so she wiped them on her skirt and brought them back.

He poured generously and she sniffed it. It smelled of the hills, of Scotland, of peat and dark afternoons such as this one was turning out to be as they sat. Through her glass she could see the flames. He got up and put more wood on to the fire and as he did so the wood spit sparks into the room, almost like on Bonfire Night. This is the first time I've felt happy in as long as I can remember, she thought.

The whisky stung her lips, set alight her tongue, and burned her throat. It then provided a glow as it went down.

'It's nice,' she said in surprise and then guilt. Her mother would have had a fit if she could have seen her.

'Cigarette?' He offered the packet.

Maddy eyed it warily and then took one and put it to her lips.

'Be careful or you'll choke,' he said, flicking the lighter open.

She didn't choke, and she thought that was probably strange since it was her first cigarette. She liked the blue smoke from it, the feel of the roll of tobacco between her lips.

She sat back in her chair and looked at him.

'So what are you doing here?'

He shrugged. And she understood even without him saying anything. They had the same problem; he was at home on his own with his dad and she was at home on her own with her mother and it was no fun. If he had friends in the village, which she doubted because he was always away, they would be with their families on Christmas Day and she had no friends because she had previously lived so far out of the village that somehow it had never worked. She had not needed anybody but her parents. It hadn't seemed odd at the time but it did now. She needed people her own age, but she could not tell her mother this.

'I like the place,' he said.

'Do you really?' Now she was impressed. Nobody had ever said that they liked her home.

'I like how it stands here by itself and the view is really good.'

You couldn't see the view any more, Maddy realized, looking at the windows. The day was fading fast, the light was leaving and soon it would not be Christmas Day any more.

'I should go.'

'Don't worry, I'll see you home,' he said, and it sounded like he meant it. It was the nicest thing she could remember anybody saying. It was like 'I'll keep you safe' and though she knew that was what women wanted men to be like, she didn't think they were. Her father must have wanted to keep her and her mother safe but instead he had died and left them. She resented that, hated the fact that he was not there, had especially hated that he was not there at Christmas for the first time ever.

'Do you miss your mother at Christmas?' she said.

He took a big swallow of whisky and then he said, 'No.'

Maddy thought she could see his mouth tremble and for the first time she wondered what his lips tasted like as he pulled heavily on the cigarette between his slim fingers. She was horrified at herself and then wanted to laugh. She was seventeen. Wasn't that what being seventeen was all about, wondering what somebody's mouth tasted like?

'I miss my dad,' she said. 'Do you get used to it?'

'No,' he said.

She wandered over to the piano and eyed it.

'Do you play?' he said.

'I used to play for my dad. I . . .' She hesitated because she hadn't told anybody this before. 'After he died I came up one night and played for him in the middle of the night. Do you think I'm mad?'

He looked at her.

'No, I think it's a nice idea and brave of you to come by yourself. I wish I'd been here. I would have come with you if you'd liked.'

'We couldn't take the piano with us, you see and . . . I used to play for him.'

'What was his favourite?'

'"Drink To Me Only With Thine Eyes".'

'Will you play it now?'

She hesitated.

'Oh, go on,' he urged her.

So she did and somehow it didn't seem wrong and daft though she knew the idea was she felt as though her dad and Sep had made some sort of connection up there in the house and it made the house dear to her. When the music stilled she went back and sat down.

'That was nice. I can see why he liked it,' Sep said.

She finished her cigarette and her whisky. 'I should go home.'

He got up and they left the fire to itself. She regretted that and wished they could have stayed. The house felt lonely, she could feel it, and she didn't want to leave the piano or her father's ghost or spirit or whatever it was, or the memories of them together, and of her mother. She lingered.

Sep had left the bottle.

'Aren't you taking that?' she said.

'It's for next time,' he said and he slipped the cigarettes and the little silver lighter into his pocket.

The fire was still blazing high. Maybe, she thought, the house will burn down with the sparks that fly from it into the air, into the sitting room when we have gone, but though they walked all the way down the hill nothing burst into flame and when she looked back in the darkness as the evening took over the land there was nothing but the black outline of the building up on the tops. She liked the idea that the fire would be dying down but not out. It would light the room for another hour or maybe more and there was something comforting about that.

'I miss it so much, you know,' she said.

'You don't have to miss it. We can go back tomorrow, and you can play the piano if you like,' he said, and she thought, yes they could. 'We can drink the rest of the whisky.'

He walked her to her door.

'When are you going back to school?' she said.

'Never,' he said.

'Aren't you? Why?'

'They decided they were better off without me.'

'What did you do?' Maddy said, suddenly breathless realizing how tall he was, how lean and how suddenly important to her.

'Nothing,' he said, 'that was the trouble.'

'You didn't go to lessons?'

'I didn't go to anything. Will I see you tomorrow?'

'Shall we go back to the house?'

'I'll be there,' he said.

The hours between now and then were nothing but an encumbrance to her. She counted them as she lay sleepless through the night and thought about him. She dreamed about the curve of his body and the glint in his dark eyes and the way that his hair fell and his hands on the glass and his lips on the cigarette and the paleness of his face and how he had looked when they spoke of his mother.

She waited, wondering when he would go to the house. She endured the morning and lunchtime though she ate nothing and then made her way back up the hill, trying not to run. When she got there the door was ready for her to push open and he was down in front of the fire in the sitting room, lighting it, and when he heard her he turned.

'I thought you might have changed your mind,' he said.

Maddy came forward as the flames began to lick the wood.

'You're good at making fires,' she said.

'I've had a lot of practice,' he said.

'Have you really?'

She knelt down beside him and he moved towards her as she did so. Then his mouth found hers and she gave a little sigh because she had spent hours and hours wondering how he would taste and what it would feel like. Now she could put her arms around his neck and give him her lips and it was wonderful.

'That was my first kiss,' she told him.

'Was it any good?' he said.

'It was bliss.'

He laughed. 'We could do it again if you like.'

She hesitated.

'I'm not going to hurt you,' he said.

'All right then.'

He took her into his arms properly, so that she felt really safe for the first time since her father had died. She knew it was silly, that in some ways it was the least safe place she had ever been, but she couldn't help wanting to be there, his body fitted so perfectly against hers, and she knew that it was what people were meant to do. Her father was dead but she must go forward and do whatever it was that she must do.

She learned about kissing while the day grew old. She could hear the fire crackling behind her. They lay down in front of it and she was too warm at one side and too cold at the other and when she told him he laughed and covered her body for warmth with his own.

'Now are you happy?' he said.

'Perfectly.'

'Really?'

'Yes, really.'

He wanted to see her on New Year's Eve.

'I don't see how I can get away,' Maddy said.

'Yes, you can. When your mother's gone to bed slide down the roof. I'll wait and catch you.'

Maddy wasn't happy with any of this. She didn't want to deceive her mother and knew that her mother had been asked nowhere on New Year's Eve. When she had been little there had been big parties at their house or other houses in the village, but when her father had got ill these had stopped as it was too far to go into the village if they had to walk back. Besides he was never well enough to enjoy them. She knew this year was different and kept waiting for her mother's friends to ask her but nobody did.

'It'll be just you and me,' Rose said.

Maddy thought how boring it would be to spend New Year's Eve with just her mother, but because Rose was so keen she did not feel she could do anything else. And, anyway, Sep was a secret. Nobody knew she was seeing him and she didn't want anybody to.

She had the feeling her mother wouldn't approve of him. It was – since Maddy had started listening to customers in the shop as she served them – the talk of the village that he had got kicked out of school The old ladies thought that he had been putting his hands on one of the maids at the school. When she told him this he laughed.

'God, I wish that was the reason.'

She thumped him. They had become such good friends over the past few days.

'Don't say that,' she said. 'And don't keep saying "God". You'll get into trouble.'

His language was what her mother would have called 'appalling' and sometimes shocked her.

'Who will I get into trouble from besides you, Miss Prim?'

That made her laugh. Their friendship had already gone beyond prim, she thought, but she turned away because she very much wished he were the kind of boy her mother would have wanted her to see. She had dreams of marrying some young man who would live in a fine house and have lots of money, but Sep invaded the visions of what she should do and what she wanted to do. She liked being with him up at the house, alone, kissing him for hours and feeling the length of his body against her.

'Did they actually say that?' he asked.

'Of course not. They wouldn't put it like that, would they? But it was what they meant.'

'Well, I didn't, so there.'

'You must have done something wrong.'

'I told you. I stopped going to things.'

'What things?'

'Everything.'

'But why?'

'Because I was fed up with it. Does it matter?'

'What does your father say?'

He tried to change the subject and moved away. They were at the house, they went there every day now and nobody seemed to notice, nobody stopped them. They were in the living room.

It was a horrible day weather-wise, the sleet had not stopped, and now it was mid-afternoon and she was very aware that she should have been helping in the shop since it was Saturday and her day off from the old ladies but she was tired of helping. She wanted to see him so badly that she kept leaving the old ladies' house in the early afternoons and escaping here and had not even been able to stop herself from coming here today, even though she was convinced her mother suspected what was going on.

He was like some kind of drug, though she didn't know anything about that, only that you got an incredible feeling when you took it and weren't happy when you didn't. He was like that to her and it made her angry now because she wasn't happy when she wasn't with him; she resented his hold over her.

'You aren't a nice boy,' she said, batting him on the arm.

'No, I'm not, and if you wanted one there are dozens who go to the church every Sunday with their parents. I'm sure any of them would have you.'

'What do you mean?'

He looked at her.

'Don't pretend you don't know how beautiful you are.'

Maddy was astonished. Nobody had even told her how pretty she was, if she was pretty at all, and she had never thought about it. For him to say she was beautiful, just like that in normal conversation, was very strange, flattering and odd somehow.

'And is that why you want me?'

'Yes, but it isn't why I like you.'

'Clever clogs,' she said, and it was not until later when she was at home that she realized he had skilfully turned away the question she most wanted to ask him.

So on New Year's Eve she did as he asked and once her mother was sleeping soundly she pulled on thick clothes, pushed back the curtains, and opened the window. She could see his shadow below.

'Come on,' he said softly.

She slid down over the roof of the back room where the goods for the shop were kept, and he caught her as she got down the one storey from there.

She liked the excitement of being out at night. She liked how he put an arm around her as they walked. She could see her breath in the cold air. The pubs were full, people were spilling out on to the pavements, and she could hear laughter and singing. Sep was naturally cautious and kept into the shadows of the buildings, cutting away from the main street as soon as he could.

They left the village and every time Maddy turned around the sky had grown bigger, the stars shining like diamonds. As they walked towards her house it made her feel wonderfully strange to be there, the dark shadow of it against the sky. She stopped.

It looked so unloved, so unwanted. Not a light showed and when she looked back now the village was so tiny, so far away, and it was a bitterly cold night up here with nothing but the sheep staring at her through the bare black trees. No sound came from the streams which usually trickled down into the Wear below. Everything was frozen.

'Listen,' he said, 'there's the church clock. It's twelve.' It chimed out the new year and they could hear the sound of people cheering across the fields.

He moved closer and she liked that, up here where she felt that the land was hers. Her ancestors had owned this place forever and ever and it felt right to be up here with him. She liked how he towered over her like a bridge between herself and the village or a wall for her to hide behind.

He kissed her. It always felt like the first time, the sweet taste and the cold night and the stars were wonderful, and the rough feel of his coat under her fingers and the warmth of his body not quite close enough. It was bliss knowing that somebody really cared about her. She felt as though they had known one another for such a long time and really it was just a few days. Maybe they had met before in some other life. She hadn't thought she believed in such things. Perhaps she did now.

He kissed her again, almost like he hadn't stopped in the first place, and his thin fingers grasped the top of her coat. It seemed to Maddy at that moment that she would never again be alone. It was like Christmas and Easter and her birthday all coming together and being the best ever time.

They went on into the house, made up the fire and sat in front of it on cushions off the old sofa. She wanted never to leave, never to have to go back down to the village again. This was their house now. It belonged to them as much as it had ever belonged to her parents or her grandparents.

'I want us to stay here always,' she said.

'We will.'

'Promise?'

'I promise.'

He kissed her and they lay down in front of the fire and

she put her hands on to the warmth of his bare skin and then wasn't happy until he was close.

'Why have you stopped?' she said when he took his warm fingers away.

'Because.'

'Don't "because".'

'Maddy . . . have you had too much to drink?'

'No. Have you?'

'No.'

'Are you sure?'

'Oh, for goodness' sake.'

'What if there's a baby?'

'Don't you want a baby?'

'I think I would.'

'Well, then.'

It was the house, she reasoned afterwards, she blamed the house. You had to blame something that you did such things, because it was not like her to do things like that normally and it was terrible when you were not married and when he was a bad boy. It made you a bad girl. How wonderful and dreadful it was to be so bad. The house was theirs now in a completely new way. Nothing would ever be the same again.

Only when the night was almost over did they go back to the village. She was so reluctant to leave. They walked down the cold fields arm in arm, and he saw her to her house and lifted her on to the sloping roof so that she could scramble across to the window. He watched her and laughed quietly as she tried to get back in. When she had succeeded he waved at her and smiled, and she watched him walk away.

He walked across the square to his house. He was not so far. Maybe from now on he would never feel far away. She loved how tall he was, she loved his dark figure going away from her, imagining if she lifted her hand she could make him come back. He was hers. There was nothing like having somebody belong to you. She had not realized how much more important it was than her father or her mother.

How strange. They had no blood together, but she felt at

that moment she would do anything to be where he was, that every evening for the rest of her life she would want to be with him. She would be jealous of everybody he loved, of everything he gave his time to. He would always be hers, had always been hers as though time meant nothing. Oh, what a gift. As she watched him disappear into the shadows beside his house she waved. He looked back and waved too, and she could feel him smiling.

On New Year's Day they ate breakfast in the tiny dining room which was their sitting room.

'Tell me, Maddy,' her mother said, 'how long have you been seeing Edgar Ward's son?'

Her mother's voice sounded like a block of wood. Maddy paused mid bite of toast and marmalade and put the slice back down on to her plate.

'How did you know?' Maddy's heart beat hard.

'Everybody knows, it would seem, except me. You didn't deign to tell me. I felt so foolish when Phoebe Robson knew more than I did about it.'

'I didn't like to tell you,' Maddy said.

'I'm not surprised. Of all the boys in the village why on earth choose that one?'

'I didn't choose him.'

'He's been expelled from school. Did you know that?'

'Yes.'

'They aren't a nice family. His mother was treated so badly by his father that she ran away.'

Rose looked as though she regretted having said this the moment it left her lips.

'She ran away? I thought she died.'

'As far as I know she did. Local gossip said she went back to the Scottish island she came from because Edgar Ward was so cold-hearted that she couldn't bear it. He wouldn't let her take her child. I can't imagine what that did to her, but that boy has had no parenting at all. He won't make a decent man and I would be grateful if you decided not to see him again.'

Her mother seemed to think that was the end of it.

'I love him.'

Her mother closed her eyes and said, 'Oh, my goodness me!'

'If you knew him, you would like him, I'm sure you would. Shall I bring him to the shop?'

'Maddy, people will talk about you. Young girls can lose their good names so easily and you cannot afford to lose yours. You have no father to help you on in life so you must be doubly careful not to cultivate the wrong kind of people. That boy is trouble. Please, consider what you're doing. There are dozens of nice boys, don't spoil your life over one wicked one.'

Wicked. Maddy was convinced he had been thrown out of school for some reason she didn't understand, and he smoked and drank and was indolent, but wicked?

'He's not,' she said.

Eight

'I've spoken to the headmaster at Wolsingham Grammar School. You can start this week,' Sep's father said.

They hadn't spoken in days. Sep had got into a routine, sort of. He saw Maddy as often as he could. Other than that, even if she was not with him, he would go up to the house and make up the fire and read and doze.

It was the new year and his father was obviously convinced he was about to make some kind of new start. It made him feel uncomfortable. He said nothing. His father obviously didn't expect an argument. He walked out of the house, clashing the front door for all the things they hadn't discussed, and went to work.

Sep didn't take any notice and just went on with what he was doing. Several days after school started his father came home in the evening, threw down some papers on the small table by the sitting room fire, and said, 'You didn't go to school.'

'I didn't say I would.' Sep didn't look up from the sofa by the fire where he had spent most of the day.

His father was silent for a moment and then he said, 'If you want to go to university—'

'I don't.'

'Why not?'

Sep was surprised at the forbearance. He didn't answer.

'You're going to do law, aren't you? You're bright enough to do it. If you could contain yourself . . .' His father stopped, no doubt perceiving the slight amusement in his voice and being surprised. 'There's no reason why you shouldn't.'

'I'm not going,' Sep said.

There was silence again, longer this time, but his father still didn't lose the patient note in his voice.

'What are you going to do?'

'I don't know yet.'

'You don't seem to do anything other than read trashy books and associate with Madeline Grant.'

That made Sep look up. 'Associate' was a new word for what they were doing.

'Do you think she's a suitable person?' his father said.

'For what?'

'I don't know. What did you have in mind?'

Well, he couldn't possibly tell his father that. He didn't think the old man had had a woman in years. He probably didn't know what to do with one.

'You're far too young to marry anybody and if you get her into trouble . . .'

It made Sep want to laugh. Into trouble. Yes, that was it. And better than associate. It made them sound like business partners of some kind.

'I haven't got her into trouble,' he said.

'Not yet.'

'I live in hope,' Sep said.

'Very funny. What are you going to do?'

'Get a job I expect.'

'Doing what?'

'I don't know.'

'You could work in my office and then later—'

'No.'

'We have offices in Durham and here. It's the family business and you are more than capable of carrying it on. If you were stupid or determined to do something else, like medicine, it would be different, but you aren't.'

'I'm not going back to school or on to university,' Sep said.

'So, you intend to sit around here, spending time with little shop girls and living off me.'

It sounded inviting, Sep thought, but the 'little shop girls' stung.

'She's not a little shop girl,' he said.

'Her father was a wastrel—'

'Her father's dead. Really dead.'

'What does that mean?' His father had one hand on the back of the sofa and Sep knew from experience that it wasn't far from the back of the sofa to him, but he didn't move.

'Not like my mother.'

His father's hand grabbed at the top of the sofa, the blood went from his knuckles.

'I never said she was dead.'

'Just as well then since she's nothing of the sort.'

'You've seen her?'

'She was living in Durham.'

His father didn't seem able to take that in though surely, Sep thought, he must have known all that time. He didn't say anything.

'Did you know?' Sep could not help asking.

'She had no right to contact you—'

'She didn't contact me. I saw her walking around the riverbanks with the woman she left you and me for.'

'She did nothing of the kind,' his father said.

'Oh, yes, she did.'

'You have no right to say things like that.'

'What then? Did you drive her away? Is that what happened?'

He didn't see the hand coming fast enough. It caught him hard around the side of the head and his father wasn't happy with that. It was the third blow that knocked him on to the floor. And even then Edgar went on smacking him round the head until Sep couldn't think straight and was curled up small with the smell of blood under his nose and the taste of it in his mouth.

'Pack your bags and get out,' his father said before he left the room. 'I don't want you in my house any more. You're just like her! You look like her and you're acting like she did. You can go and live with your little shop girl.'

The thing was, Sep thought as he lay there, that the old man probably didn't mean it and wouldn't expect him to leave just as he had no doubt not expected his mother to leave. After all, where would he go? He had no money, no friends.

There was a noise in the doorway as somebody hesitated there. His father had not cared in his fit of temper that Mrs Herries, the housekeeper, was making the dinner in the kitchen and would have had to be extremely hard of hearing not to know what was going on.

'Oh, laddie,' she said, in an attempt at lightness with sympathy, 'what has he done to you?'

'I'm fine,' Sep said.

'Do you want the doctor?'

'No, of course I don't,' and he sat up to prove he could do it.

'It's a wild temper he has on him,' she said, 'for a legal man.'

That made Sep smile as though the profession did not allow for emotions. He couldn't imagine what any of them would say to Dr Robson and besides he was only bruised and shaken.

He got up, wiping the blood away from his face, nose and mouth.

'You wouldn't lend me some money so that I could go to Durham and get a job, would you?' he said.

'That's not a good idea.'

'I'll send you it back.'

'It's late and it's dark now. Have you nowhere you can go?'

He shook his head.

'You could come home with me.'

Sep was grateful to her though he couldn't imagine how his father would react if he went home and stayed with Mr and Mrs Herries. She would lose her job for a start. Mr Herries had been a quarryman until he badly damaged his leg and hadn't worked in years so she couldn't afford to lose her job, which made it all the better that she was prepared to sacrifice it for him.

'That's very nice of you,' he said, 'but I couldn't.'

'Maybe it'll blow over with your dad,' she said.

'He wants me to stop seeing Maddy.' Sep didn't pretend Mrs Herries and all the rest of the village wouldn't know.

'She's a fine wee lassie,' Mrs Herries said, obviously forgetting she hadn't been to Scotland in twenty years since she'd left to marry Mr Herries.

'Do you think she is?' he said, eager for somebody to say something kind.

'Och, yes.'

'I'd better go and pack.'

'Wait until the morning.'

'Will you lend me some money in the morning?'

'Aye, I will,' she said. 'Mr Herries has a few pennies put by. If you're still of the same mind tomorrow we'll help you out. Are you going to have your supper now?'

She fussed so he ate. His father had gone to the office next door and the lights blazed until it was almost midnight.

The following morning Sep packed his clothes and a few books – they were heavy so not many – and he stayed in his room until his father had gone to work Then he stood up, smoking a cigarette he had taken as he always did from his father's stash in the court cupboard. He had packed a great many of those and a bottle of single malt and, waiting until he saw Maddy leave to go to the old ladies' house, he called out to her across the square. She stopped and looked hard at him.

'What happened to you?' she said.

He hadn't thought it was so bad, but the look on her face told him otherwise.

'Does it show?'

'Of course it shows. Have you been fighting?'

'Not exactly.'

'You shouldn't. My mother thinks badly enough of you to begin with,' she said. 'What was it about?'

'I'm leaving.'

She didn't understand, he could see that she didn't. She just went on looking at him and he thought, no, people so rarely left the dale that she didn't believe him. Families had been there for hundreds of years, they didn't go anywhere.

'What do you mean?'

'I mean I'm going into Durham to find a job.'

'You don't have to leave to do that.'

'My father seems to think it's a good idea.'

She didn't believe that either for a few moments.

'Is he putting you out?'

'No, he just lost his temper,' Sep said.

'He hit you?' Her voice was full of astonishment as though men never hit their sons. What world did she live in? 'Are you leaving home because he hit you?'

'No, I'm not. I just want to get away from here.'

'Whatever do you mean?' Maddy said.

Sep didn't answer. She was staring.

'How many times did he hit you to get you into such a state?'

'Does it matter?'

'Of course it matters. Look at you. He shouldn't do that.'

Neither of them spoke for a few moments and then she said slowly, 'Was it because of me?'

'No.' He spoke too quickly, and she was not reassured.

'It was. Everybody knows. He doesn't like me . . .'

'He doesn't know you. And it wasn't because of you. He wants me to go back to school and to go on to university and I'm not going to.'

'Why ever not?'

'I can't. I don't want to go on living with him and I can't stay here.'

'But . . .' She didn't say 'what about us' though he thought he heard the words and her face took on an immediate misery. He thought she was going to cry.

'Will you come with me?'

She stared even harder.

The cold wind was blowing his hair about. She didn't like it. She didn't like the reckless look in his eyes or the bitter line of his mouth.

'You shouldn't talk like that. It's just . . . just because of what happened.'

'Don't you want to get away?'

'I can't leave,' she said.

'Why not?'

'Because of my mother. My father has just died, I can't go and leave her, and anyway, I assumed you were going back to school, that some school would be daft enough to take you and you would go to university. Wasn't that what you intended to do?'

'I'll find a job.'

'Doing what? Do you know how to do anything?'

He didn't answer that.

'Please don't leave. Surely your dad didn't mean it.'

'I don't want to be here any more.'

She wanted to tell him that he couldn't go, that she couldn't manage without him, that he was the one good thing left in her life, that if she had to go on without him . . . If he wouldn't stay here without somebody imploring him not to then he must go, but nobody should hit anybody like that so he couldn't stay, she knew he couldn't.

'Please don't go and leave me here,' she said.

'I'm sorry,' he said, 'there's nothing else I can do. I'd be happy to take you with me.'

'What would I do in Durham?'

'I don't know.'

'And how would we live?'

'I don't know that either. I just don't want to leave without you.' He got hold of her, kissed her, made it almost impossible for her to imagine any kind of life without him. 'I can't stay here now. Come with me. I'll make it right, you know I will. Don't make me go by myself. I want you with me.'

'I can't.' Maddy drew back, beginning to cry. She couldn't bear the idea of him not being there and would have done almost anything to keep him with her.

She put her arms around his neck and clung, kissing him over and over.

'I'm going now.' He pulled back.

'No!'

'Yes, I am. You've made your choice.'

'And you've made yours.' Maddy's voice was too loud for her ears, too despairing. She had lost her temper and though she tried hard to get it back she couldn't because the crying got in the way and she still had her arms around his neck. She wanted to plead further, but she couldn't. It took all she had to take her arms from his neck and stand back so that she wasn't stopping him.

He didn't say anything. He just threw his half-smoked cigarette into the gutter and then he turned and walked off. It made her cry even harder. She wanted to run after him but she had the awful feeling that no matter what she said or did it wouldn't make any difference. She felt sick and lonely and the way that she had felt when her father had died. She couldn't go home, she couldn't move for a very long time and only the wind, which swept down from the fells, eventually dried her tears.

When she got back to the house her mother said, 'We're going to Mr and Mrs Philips' party this afternoon, to the vicarage. You haven't forgotten?'

'I'm not going,' Maddy said, stumbling up the stairs.

'Maddy?' Her mother peered up the stairs, but she went into her room and slammed the door.

It was only then that she remembered her mother hardly ever went anywhere any more and for that reason alone she changed into her best dress. She could not think, she did not want to think any more, she only wanted something to do which was normal and ordinary so that she wouldn't have to think about Sep leaving.

Her mother came upstairs. 'You are going then?'

'Of course.' She did her best to smile.

'What's going on?'

'It's Sep. He's leaving. He's going to Durham.'

Her mother looked so relieved, but she went over and said, 'I'm so sorry for you, Maddy,' which made things better than they had been in a long time.

She didn't say any of those awful things like 'you'll find somebody else' or 'you'll find somebody better' or 'he wasn't right for you'. She just cuddled her and it was the best thing she could have done.

'It will work out eventually if it's supposed to,' Rose said.

'What if I never see him again?'

Her mother laughed a little but it was sympathetic.

'Durham isn't that big,' she said.

'He might go further away.'

'He might,' and her mother kissed her.

She didn't tell her mother he had asked her to go with him and her mother must be very glad he had gone. She probably hoped they would never see him again.

It was a big house, the vicarage, but not as big as their house had been and quite different. It was square stone and rather forbidding, standing as it did in the shadow of the graveyard and away from the clusters of houses. It was though it was not really part of the village but belonged only to the church and its surroundings.

There were a great many trees which meant that it was in shade all day during the summer and flowers would not grow in profusion around it. It was mostly green all year round with stuff like ferns that didn't seem, as far as she could tell knowing nothing about such things, to mind there not being any sun in the vicarage garden.

Inside was even gloomier because when it was a windy day the trees seemed to move their shadows across the rooms. She could remember as a child being brought here and having the big branches looking in at the sitting-room windows and being afraid of them though she knew that she shouldn't be, that they could not harm her.

It was not a small group of people. A great many people had been asked to the vicarage that afternoon and it was not that bad. Small twinkles of sunlight came through the branches of the trees as though they were playing peepo as small children did when you picked them up, hiding in against your shoulder and then looking out.

She and her mother went inside where Mrs Philips was pouring tea and displaying her daughter, newly married, to the neighbourhood. She had married a businessman in Newcastle and had a fine house there, so Mrs Philips said, and Maddy did not doubt the truth of it as it was sure to be something important because Mrs Philips seemed very pleased.

They had not been invited to the wedding. She thought

her mother minded about that because they were old friends and the Robsons had been invited, but her mother had said nothing about it so she had not thought. She did now.

Penny had been married at the church, her father had officiated, her brother, John, had given her away. Like a bloody parcel, Maddy thought savagely. They had heard all the details.

Penny wore a very pretty dress today and looked happy as she distributed plates of little cakes to the various ladies who sat on the sofas around the big room. They laughed and asked her how married life was going, and she laughed and said all the right things.

Maddy noticed the vicar's piano in the corner beyond everybody. It was nothing like the piano she had had at home, that was a relief somehow, but it was still a piano. Quite a big one with the sort of lid that came up and stood on a gold broomstick to show off the keys or maybe the better for the notes to come out. There was no music on it and nobody played it or noticed it. It was well polished and the light fell on it as it fell on nothing else in the room and her fingers itched to play.

'Would you play for us, Maddy?'

Mr Philips was there, smiling.

She had not realized she was still watching the piano. She wanted to etch it on her mind so that when she was lying in bed that night she would recall the dark colour, how creamy white the keys were, where the sunlight fell upon the lid and how the little brass feet stuck into the carpet as though it was heavy. She longed for the piano, to hear its sound, to find the notes upon the air so that the atmosphere in the room would lift, so that the noise of people talking, saying such ordinary things, would be drowned out by the beauty of the music however simple.

She had played for her mother and for her father and for Sep. Only her mother was left. She went over to the piano. She could no longer resist the appeal of it standing there and looking so inviting. She lifted the lid from the keys and it was a bit like somebody taking the top off a biscuit tin when all the biscuits were chocolate and delicious. There the notes lay and she knew how they worked and what they would sound like.

She sat down, put her fingers on the keys and the sounds began to come out. She had been right, she could not hear what was being said probably about how Sep had left his home and his father. People did not know how his father had treated him and how his mother had not been there for him. She did not have to listen to the village gossip.

She had never cared what people did and now the notes were lifting themselves into the air and floating across the room and she played on and the sound filled the whole of the vicarage until there was nobody but herself, not even her mother. She played 'Drink To Me Only With Thine Eyes' and she thought Sep could hear her even though he had probably already left for Durham. He would always hear her playing and she would always play for him even though she hated him for going, hated him for leaving her. She thought she would miss him more than she could bear.

Nine

The first thing to do was to find somewhere to stay and Sep found a house with rooms to let in Ravensworth Terrace off Claypath, which was up a hill from the market place in the direction of Sunderland.

It was a neat terraced house, one in a long street, with bay windows which snaked up the hill. Mrs Kennedy, the landlady, showed him into a tiny bedroom at the back which looked out at an alleyway and a brick wall. It was nothing like the bedroom he was used to – just a single bed, a chest of drawers, a wardrobe and nothing much else – but he was to have breakfast and an evening meal there. He was surprised at how expensive it was, so although he would have liked something better he was aware that he had no job, no money and must be careful and he said he would take it. It seemed respectable enough and that was the important thing at present.

There was a bathroom across the landing. He left his bag there, she gave him a key, and he went back into town, looking for something to do, calling at various offices, though bypassing his father's offices in Elvet.

He tried not to panic. Mrs Herries had given him enough for his bus fare, his lodgings and a little left though it would buy him nothing more than a meal in one of the grubby looking cafes he had passed by. He must find something to do today and then he would not be able to eat except at the boarding house for a week or a fortnight or however long it was before people were paid.

There didn't seem to be much work. He had hoped for an office but none of the offices anywhere had signs for jobs in the windows. He thought maybe they didn't and started calling in, but people mainly just looked at him. He went to the shops and realized from the shopkeepers' hard stares and sharp questions that his accent was getting in his way and maybe his manner too because he was unused to this way of life. He thought that perhaps he wasn't humble enough, though whether humble would do when people were naturally mistrustful he wasn't sure. Durham was such a small city, maybe you had to know somebody to get a job or people had to know who you were.

Eventually he came across the office of one of the pits on the edge of the town out towards Hartlepool and ventured in there since there was a sign in the window which said they needed a clerk. The man looked suspiciously at him when he enquired. Sep modified his accent immediately and became thick Durham.

'You don't look very old to me.'

'I'm almost eighteen.'

'Can you read and write?'

Sep felt like saying, 'I wouldn't be here if I couldn't,' but he nodded and waited.

The man got up and went into the inside office through a glass door and after a low murmured conversation which Sep could not make out he came back.

'Go in.'

An older man was inside. And he asked the same question about reading and writing and Sep couldn't help saying with pride, he thought afterwards, 'I can do Latin and French too.'

'Well, that'll be a big help,' the man said. Sep saw the humour, smiled and felt encouraged.

He said, 'I'm good at maths.'

'That's even better. Never worked at a pit office though?'

'Not yet. Will you give me a chance?'

'You haven't done something you shouldn't?'

'No.'

'Not running away? I'm not going to get some lady coming here crying that you fell out with your dad, because you have a posh accent.'

Sep thought he had hidden it well. This man had seen through him.

'My father knows I'm in Durham looking for work and I don't have a mother.'

It was the first time he had ever said so, the first time it had really been true.

'Some lass then you're trying to get away from?'

It was true but not relevant here.

'No,' Sep said.

Have you been down a pit?'

'No.'

'You're big. Are you frightened of small spaces?'

'I don't know. I was never in one. You don't want me hewing down there, do you?'

'We have skilled men to do that.' The man smiled to soften the blow and Sep smiled back.

'All right, you can come underground with me. If you don't scream for your mother I might let you stay,' the man said.

Sep wanted to say that he hadn't screamed for his mother even when he was a little boy and had thought she had died so he was hardly likely to do it now and then they went to where the pit wheel spun and there was the winding gear and the cage which took the miners to the bottom of the shaft, closed into a very small dark space, and then fell so fast that you left your stomach above your head when it landed. He was in a darkness such as he had never been in before. It was thick and scary at the bottom of the shaft and he soon saw what Mr Gregson meant because as they went into the tunnels the roof was so low that even a medium-sized man could not have straightened up.

'You all right?' Mr Gregson prompted him.

'Yes, I'm fine.'

Sep thought he would not have said he was frightened even if he was wetting himself from fear. He thought further and knew that there was only one kind of person who went down into places like this, where the men toiled to take the coal from low seams and there were only little pockets of light. The timbers creaked which was hardly reassuring but to his surprise he was fascinated rather than anything else and as long as he was careful and remembered how tall he was he was not afraid.

The men down there spent full shifts below ground and they were not bothered though they knew, everybody knew, that it was a very dangerous thing to do, that many Durham pitmen had died, that pits had explosions, roof falls, flooding and that what every pitman dreaded was to be caught down there behind a fall and die of hunger and thirst. It must be, Sep thought, one of the hardest deaths of all.

He was not even particularly relieved when they got back to the surface and into Mr Gregson's tiny office because he was more afraid that he would not be able to do the office work and that he wouldn't find any job at all and have to go back to his father. He could not think of a worse fate.

'You still want the job?'

'Yes, I do, as long as you'll show me what to do.'

'It wouldn't be much good if I didn't,'Mr Gregson said and added, 'you do know it's just you and me up here, don't you, that you have to be on hand all the time and that if there is a problem we might have to go down there?'

Have you ever been in an accident?'

'Two, and I'm still here.' Mr Gregson smiled encouragingly. 'You can have a week and whatever happens I'll pay you for that week, but if at the end of it I decide you aren't what I'm looking for you'll have to go. Do you understand?'

'Yes. I'll do my best,' Sep said.

'Good,' and then he was shown in to the little office outside.

'This'll be yours. If there's anything you don't understand let me know.'

He explained about the work coming in and the work going out and the orders and the invoices and the wages and then he showed Sep around, who was rather taken with the idea of having a whole office to himself. It felt stupidly powerful. It was a small operation as pits went and Sep was glad of that too because it would give him a chance to work out what was going on and to understand it all quickly.

The pitmen coming and going on shift called out as they

came in; the pit wheel and the winding gear rumbling; the buildings at the top, including the office. There was something about it all which Sep instantly liked. He wasn't sure whether it was the camaraderie. He went back to his little office and put coal on the fire.

'Don't stint yourself,' Mr Gregson said with a grin. 'It's free, you know.'

'Shall I do yours as well then?'

'Aye, do. I keep forgetting and letting it go out. Have you got somewhere to stay?'

'I found a room in Ravensworth Terrace.'

'Good,' Mr Gregson said.

Maddy kept on working for the two old ladies and when she was not at work she helped her mother with the shop. She was glad to have so much to do, it meant she didn't have time to think about Sep and she managed to conjure up anger against him and the anger consumed all her other feelings.

She told herself he could not really have cared about her or he would not have gone. When people talked and said he was a bad lad for leaving his home and his dad she wanted to defend him and had to stop herself from talking about him. There was nothing between them any more and she must get on with her life.

She took the various orders around to people in the village. She was glad of an excuse to get away because she didn't like serving in the shop. She helped to organize the back room, ordered goods, did the books in the evenings and dusted, washed and restocked the shelves.

She washed the floor late at night because she couldn't bear to see how tired her mother had become with everything that had happened and also washed the windows two or three times a week, especially if it rained. She was proud to know that the shop looked as good as it possibly could.

She also helped with the housework, the washing and ironing, keeping the fires going and sometimes the cooking. Her only escape was on Sunday afternoons when she had finished washing the dinner dishes and she would go for a walk. Her mother never asked her where she was going, now that Sep had left, Maddy thought. She had nothing to worry about. Maddy did not go back to the old house once Sep had left and she did not regret her piano there. She thought she would never want to play the piano again. She walked around by the river, it was safe there, no memories to intrude.

'I should go to evening classes,' she said brightly to her mother that spring.

'Don't you work sufficiently?' her mother said wearily.

'I could type the letters and bills and everything. It would look so much more professional. You remember Miss Primrose?'

Jane Primrose had taught mathematics at the local schools for years and was now teaching bookkeeping, typing and shorthand at the village hall in the evenings.

'It would be good for you to have something besides work, not as well as,' her mother said, 'but if you want to you should do it.'

Luckily the classes were on Tuesdays and Thursdays and these were the slowest days at the shop so her mother was not too tired to cope alone with everything else in the evenings.

The old hardware store in Sweet Wells was closing down. That was the rumour. The shop was empty for only a few days and then to Maddy's dismay she saw that it was to become another grocery shop. The village was not big enough for theirs, the Store and another and the people who moved in were a young man and his wife.

They had no children. Maddy watched carefully from the big window at the front of the shop. Each of them would have as much energy as she and her mother put together, more, and they would have no other responsibilities. They were young and keen.

It was brightly painted outside and their names, J & T Wilson, were written in flourishing letters over the top of the door. It was a bigger building than theirs and also, and she thought this was very clever, they opened a little tea shop to one side, just inside the shop, with a few tables and chairs where weary shoppers could have tea and home-made fruitcake, scones or toasted teacakes, all made by Mrs Wilson.

Even from across the square Maddy could smell the baking in the early morning and since they opened earlier than everybody else, people began calling in to collect bread first thing in the morning. Maddy had the feeling that many a local housewife passed Mrs Wilson's baking off as her own. Mrs Wilson had her own dairy and here she produced wonderful butter and cheese and she kept hens so that she could sell fresh eggs.

Mrs Wilson made coffee for the mid-morning shoppers. The smell of that coupled with the bread brought people in from the small villages when the weather was fine. She made marmalade early in the year and pink sweets for Valentine's Day and special cards. In the summer she sold vegetables which Mr Wilson grew in the big patch in the back garden behind the shop and even flowers and tomatoes and cucumbers in the late summer which they grew in their greenhouse.

Later in the year Mrs Wilson sold them sticky toffee apples in the autumn, plum jam for those who didn't make their own, and mistletoe and holly which she collected from the hedgerows and fields, and Christmas cards and Christmas cakes and plum puddings which she had made.

She put silver and gold decorations in the windows and she made cards and sold those and soap and sold that, in little boxes or baskets prettily done up with ribbons. Mrs Wilson, Maddy thought, was a very clever woman. She got local women to knit garments to be sold as presents and a woman from Westgate who was a quilter to make special baby quilts and another woman from Eastgate who did embroidery to do tray cloths.

The shop soon had three departments, the groceries, the gifts and the tea shop and Mr Wilson employed help: a boy with a bike for the orders, a woman to make tea and coffee and serve out chocolate cake and coffee and walnut cake and fruit cake with cherries and another woman in the drapery department with the quilts and special embroidered pillowcases – you could have your initials on them if you wanted. What a luxury.

There were pullovers with snow scenes or reindeer for the children and Mrs Wilson even bought in toys so that the children clamoured for them when they went shopping with their mothers.

Maddy was half inclined to go over and ask Mrs Wilson for a job and then she panicked. What would happen when people didn't come to their shop any more? Mr Wilson had begun undercutting their prices and sometimes now there would not be anybody in the shop for an hour. She found herself with time to look about and regret what could not be.

The takings were well down even before Christmas. She had thought that this Christmas would be better than last but it wasn't; she became afraid of what the future might hold. What if they should lose the shop? What would they do? It was somehow ironic that everybody but them seemed able to afford special things from the Wilsons' shop for Christmas.

On Christmas Eve she stood alone and watched people going in and out of the new shop and waited and waited for it to be late enough to close up. She locked the door, turned over the closed sign and went wearily up the stairs. Her mother had made a stew earlier. They gathered around the table and had rabbit stew and bread and it was in that moment that she thought it wasn't enough.

'I'm going to find a job after Christmas. Miss Primrose thinks I have sufficient secretarial skills to do so.'

'But who will run the shop?' her mother said.

'We won't have the shop much longer.'

Her mother sighed and then managed a smile.

'I could envy Mrs Wilson, she's so clever,' she said. 'She's a much better shopkeeper than I could ever be. It's brave of you to offer to go out and work. I don't know what we will do if the shop closes. Mr Felix will probably sell it or get somebody else in to do something Mrs Wilson can't do.'

'If there is anything like that,' Maddy said and they both tried to smile.

'Don't worry, I'll find something,' Maddy said.

They had their dinner and after that Maddy made an excuse to go upstairs and read by the oil lamp she took with her. She liked that time best of all, when the day was over and there was no point in worrying about what might happen now. Sometimes she read far into the night and lost herself in people who had problems she didn't have.

It did not snow. It was not going to be a white Christmas. It was going to be a different Christmas. She went to the library for her books. There were hundreds of books. It was such a comfort to know that. It was all the escape she had.

Ten

Black's Foundry. The name was written up in big appropriately black letters on the gate. Maddy had been to so many places and been turned away and she had almost lost hope. She had gone to big shops where they had offices, and accountants and solicitors and businessmen and they looked at her and saw a young girl and would have nothing more to do with her.

She had been determined not to give in. She was good at office work, she had proved it to Miss Primrose by being the best in the class. Women were taken on at business places, girls very often, she had discovered, were not. If this did not work out she was not sure what she would do.

She was determined to be in Durham too and after this she might have to look for something in the dale where everybody knew her and business people were not keen on taking on people they knew in case they talked about their business. Miss Primrose had told her that. It had been her main reason for looking in Durham for a job.

Men were moving about outside and inside big sheds but she could see further along on the right-hand side what looked to her like an office. The door was open. She was going to knock, but it seemed such a silly thing to do. Inside the door was a large office. It was very untidy. In the heart of it a man was going through some papers.

He was about the same age as her dad would have been and that was nice and not at the same time because she missed him so much but she felt comfortable with men his age. He wore an old suit. It had been quite a good suit at one time, she thought, but it was so covered in dust that you couldn't even tell what colour it had been, just that it fitted him perfectly so it had been made for him.

He was quite tall and not very fat and even when he bent over as he was doing now the suit still looked good. He wore a hat as though he had just come indoors. The hat was also grey with dust. His whole demeanour was one of frustration, irritation even.

Maddy hesitated in the doorway. He looked up briefly when he heard her. He had green eyes. He said politely, in spite of the fruitless search and in a very posh accent, 'Hello. Can I help?'

'I'm looking for some work.'

'It's a steel foundry. We don't employ women.'

'No, I . . . I meant here in the office.'

He didn't reply and she became tired of waiting.

'What are you looking for?'

'It's an order and I can't remember the numbers on it. For Wests.'

She moved further into the office and to the far end of the desk where he was looking and miraculously somehow there it was on the top of a huge pile of papers. She handed it to him.

He looked surprised, pleased.

'Oh, well done,' he said and set off towards the door. Then he seemed to remember her and stopped. 'Can you type?'

'Yes.'

'Do accounts?'

'I worked in my mother's shop.'

'All right, you're hired. I'll give you a month and we'll see how you get on.'

'You will pay me?'

He looked at her and his eyes lit. He laughed. His face was really nice when he laughed, it crinkled up and he was brown as though he liked being outside.

'Don't worry,' he said, 'everybody gets paid,' and he turned around and walked out at speed.

Maddy stood still. She couldn't believe he had just left her there. She could be anybody. She could take the petty cash.

She could steal something. She looked around. She felt powerful, like she was a queen and this was her domain. Another man came in, short, stocky, also wearing dusty clothes.

'Mr Black about?'

'He's gone into the works, I think.'

'Fettling shop?' he guessed and went out again. Then somebody else came in. Another workman.

'Who're you?' he asked.

'I'm the new secretary.'

'About time,' he said. 'Mr Black?'

'Fettling shop,' she said and he went out too.

The office had three desks, several filing cabinets, a large black typewriter on the desk nearest to the door, which she imagined would be hers, and the desks and window ledges were covered in paperwork.

There was, down a corridor, another small office and this too was untidy with unopened reams of paper stacked behind the door and various files too, as though everything was overflowing.

Maddy went back into the main office and opened the first filing cabinet she came to. It wouldn't open properly as it was jammed full with papers. The others were the same and when she went through the desk drawers she soon saw why Mr Black didn't worry about anybody stealing anything. The cash box was not locked and it was empty.

Further explorations showed her that whatever filing system there had been had largely been ignored. It had been some time, she thought, since anybody had run the office. She didn't know where to start, there was so much to do.

By five o'clock it was dark. Mr Black came in at a quarter to six and passed the big clock on the wall. He paused and then said, 'I had forgotten about you. You should have gone long since. How are you getting home?'

'The bus—'

'No, no, no. It's late and it's dark. I'll take you home. Get your things.'

He locked the office and they got into his car and he drove her out of the town and through the pit villages and into the dale.

'Have you learned anything today?' he said, making conversation.

Maddy instantly liked that about him. Most people didn't bother. He was a proper gentleman, she thought, like her dad had been.

'That your office hasn't been properly looked after for a very long time,' she said, and that made him laugh.

When they reached the village Maddy thanked him and got out.

'What time in the morning, Mr Black?'

'Nine. Good evening, Miss Grant.'

Miss Grant. It made her sound so important. She ran off to the house, waving as he turned the car around. She watched the car all the way down the road and away until it was out of sight.

She had never thought she would run an office. There was nobody in it but the two of them and he was in the works a lot of the time. Sometimes he went into the little office, if he had somebody private to see or if he had to think particularly hard about something but mostly they sat in the big office together or she was there alone.

She did not feel lonely, she had never spent much time by herself before and enjoyed it and she was proud that he thought her capable. It took several weeks to sort the filing into a new system, then ordered it, and after that a day-to-day routine took over.

First of all she would open the post and then they would go through it together and he would tell her what letters he wanted sending and what she should say in them, then they would talk about the orders and the invoices and after that she would do the typing.

She kept the books so that they knew what they owed and who owed them and when the orders should be delivered. They had their own lorries to do the deliveries with Black's Foundry written on the side and she gradually learned about the various processes in the works, how the castings were made, the ingredients for the steel mixed and heated and poured into moulds and cooled, the designs for them, the shipyards they went to be fitted on to the ships and she got to know the men who owned the shipyards because they came to the works or they sent their top workmen to discuss what was being done and she soon recognized the names of the shipyards at Sunderland and Newcastle.

She liked going into the works to find him when there were important telephone calls. The men would smile or speak to her and she liked the way they dealt with the everyday work. The men who came in before five to fire up the furnace – the furnace men were so important but then every man had an important job and they were proud of what they did and she was pleased to be there, among the sand and the heat and the noise.

She made up the men's wages in the brown pay packets and handed them out on Friday afternoons when they lined up for their wages. They were always most respectful to her. She thought Mr Black was wonderful. He never let her get the bus home on dark nights as he said you never knew who was about. She was rather sorry when the light nights came and she could get the bus home. If it rained badly he would still take her home.

She soon grew used to the office life and began to relax. The little money the shop still made and her new job kept them and because she was working her mother stopped worrying, she could see by the way that her face cleared. The shop was soon just something for her mother to do so that she would think less about her father and try to live in the present. It was pleasant for a while just to go on with what they were doing. They could not afford anything expensive but it did not matter.

Her mother began to eat better and sometimes Maddy would awaken during the night and not hear her mother moving about. At one time her mother would never have slept the night through, but as the months went by she began to do so and because there were no major problems they grew to appreciate the day-to-day happenings, the walks on Sundays if the weather was fine, sitting around the fire, reading or playing simple games when the nights were dark, the coming of the seasons.

When you had gone through so much, Maddy thought, you took nothing for granted. She thanked God for each day when nothing went wrong, but she had learned not to expect very much. She did not wake up thinking everything would be all right that day, she did not dare.

Sep worked long hours but he didn't mind. There was nothing else to do. He had no money to go anywhere and made no friends. The pitmen regarded him as an outsider and he understood that. Mr Gregson was much older than he was and had a wife and family. There was no one to spend time with.

He bought books, they were his only luxury and he needed something to while away the evening hours before he went to bed. There was a stall in the covered-in market where you could buy books and then get money for bringing them back and buy new ones. It worked quite well and he got to know the old man who ran the bookstall so he started keeping the kind of books Sep liked.

Weekends were difficult but Mr Gregson was always in the office on Saturday mornings and though he did not expect Sep to be there, he went. Mr Gregson thought it was diligence and did not realize it was loneliness.

Sundays were for taking walks along the riverbanks, trying not to remember the day he had seen his mother or the years he had spent at school there. He would read in the shade of a tree or on Palace Green in the sunshine if it was a fine day. If it rained he would lie on his bed. The other residents in Mrs Kennedy's house were four men but they were all a lot older than he was. They went to the pub every night and the house was quiet. They rarely bothered talking to him or much to one another when they were in the house. They just ate their stew or their pie and got on with their lives.

One fine day, when Sep had been in the office for so long that he needed some fresh air and it was cooler in the early evening, he had gone for a long walk and was just passing the entrance to Black's Foundry when he thought he saw somebody he knew leaving the office.

The foundry would have been shut at teatime and it was now well after six, but he heard her voice and knew that it was Maddy. Nobody else sounded like her. She was cheerful, calling goodbye as she came out of the gates. He stayed back, he didn't know why, just that he was aware she might not be glad to see him and he was so confused at seeing her that he didn't know what to do.

She set off down the street. He followed her all the way to the bus station and watched her climb on the bus which went to Bishop Auckland where she would no doubt change buses to go back to the dale. He couldn't believe she was working here in Durham. He was so pleased but didn't know whether to get in touch since he had left her so abruptly and didn't think she would want anything to do with him.

He couldn't sleep for thinking about what he might do. She wouldn't know if he didn't contact her, but he wanted to contact her so much that he could not stop himself.

The following day he left the pit office just after half past five which was his official leaving time. Mr Gregson looked up in surprise because he never left then, he was always later, but he could hardly object, considering all the hours Sep did without complaint.

Sep would have liked to leave before then but he didn't want to explain or lie because he was no longer sure he was really going to see her, that he would have enough nerve to walk through the gates of Black's and into the office. Would she want to see him? Would she tell him to go away?

His heart pounded and he almost turned and ran, but he knew that if he didn't see her he wouldn't be able to sleep and he would be disgusted at his own cowardice. He made himself take leaden steps to Black's, calling himself names all the way.

Maddy was just about to put the cover on her typewriter and go home when the office door went. She smiled as she looked up because she had learned that a smile always helps, especially when somebody wants something at almost half past six.

The smile went rigid on her face. A tall, dark, young man she hadn't seen for a year was standing in the doorway. It was Sep. She stared. He was wearing a suit nearly as shabby as Mr Black's and it was not nearly as well made. He was thin, his hair was cut very short and his eyes seemed bigger to her than she had remembered.

'Hello, Maddy,' he said. 'I thought I might have missed you, that you would have already left to go home.' It seemed he was about to say more from nervousness and then realized and shut up. He managed to look shamefaced and his voice quivered.

She was amazed at his presence.

'Where did you spring from?' she said.

'I'm working in town. I wondered if you would like to go out somewhere.'

'Working here?'

'Well, not here. Up on the road to Bowburn almost out of town.'

She said nothing; he was such a shock to her.

'I have to get the bus home.'

'Couldn't you get a later bus?'

'My mother would worry.'

He didn't ask again, as though it had taken everything he had to come here, to say so, and Maddy wished in a way that she had not made her mind up so abruptly.

At that moment Mr Black called her through into his small office. He was seated behind his desk but had obviously heard the conversation.

He said softly, 'I could take you home later if you want to spend some time with the young man.'

Maddy blushed.

'We're old friends from home,' she said.

'You wouldn't be any later than usual if you went out for an hour. I think you've just missed the bus you often catch.'

'Mr Black—'

'You never go anywhere,' he said. 'I know it isn't my business but just for once . . . your mother is used to you being later, I keep you back so often.'

Maddy wished the heat in her face would go down but it didn't.

'I don't know whether I want to see him,' she explained.

'Take your time,' Mr Black said, fiddling with the papers on his desk. He asked her one or two questions about the order which had just arrived and she thought he only did so that she would have another moment or two.

'All right then,' she said, 'if you're sure you don't mind running me home.'

'I don't mind at all,' Mr Black said, smiling gently in encouragement.

She went back into the office.

'I can stay for a little while,' she said.

They walked to the County and had tea. It was the only thing she could think to ask for and then she worried that he could not afford to bring her to a fashionable place like this. He looked so poor and the County was full of people with posh voices and the women who waited on them wore uniforms. The funny part about it was that Sep was quite at home there which of course he would be with his background.

He had no difficulty at all in attracting the waitresses' attention and was polite and smiling and the two girls on duty nearly broke their necks getting to him.

It was a pleasant evening in spring. The river beyond the windows was busy on its way to Sunderland and the trees enhanced the look of the towpath, in full bud and about to burst into leaf.

'What would you like?' he said.

Maddy scanned the menu for the cheapest thing but everything was very dear, she thought, which it would be in Durham's best hotel. She decided on tea and he said, 'You can have a drink, you know.'

That reminded her uncomfortably of the whisky they had drunk when they were together at her house up on the tops and of things they had done there and she hid her scarlet face in the menu for as long as she could.

'Tea will be fine, and a scone would be nice if they're still serving them.'

He ordered tea and sandwiches and scones.

'Where are you living?' Maddy asked him.

'I have a room in a boarding house. The upper end of Ravensworth Terrace. It's small, but it's OK, and I get my breakfast and supper there.'

'It doesn't sound like much fun. What are you doing?'

'Working in a colliery office. I like it.' He sounded so defensive to Maddy.

'Is there a future in that?'

'I have no idea. I don't care much about the future. It takes me all my time to manage the present.'

'You don't come home.'

'There's nothing to come home for.'

That stung and he had meant it to, she thought.

'What about your father?'

My father doesn't want me there.'

'You should be at university. You were clever.'

Sep concentrated on his egg sandwich and didn't reply to that.

'How is your mother?' he asked.

'We manage.'

'It's hard?'

She told him about the Wilsons' shop and the problems it had caused and then she could not help saying, 'I wish you hadn't left,' and then because that made her sound vulnerable she added, 'Your father has nobody.'

Sep looked across the table at her.

'Why should I care?'

'Because you had the chance of a future if you had stayed at home and had completed your last year at school. What have you got now?' She had meant to say this, she knew he couldn't have stayed with his father treating him badly, but for the first time ever she couldn't find the right words to say to him.

'I could be a pit manager.'

'Mr Black says they'll nationalize the mines.'

'They'll still need managers for them. What's wrong with that?'

'You could have been a solicitor.'

'Whatever gave you that idea?'

'You could have done law. Your dad would have been proud of you.'

'He would never have been proud of me,' Sep said, 'and it's a stupid reason for doing anything. Would you like another cup of tea?'

'No, thank you. I have to go. I told Mr Black I'd be no more than an hour.'

They walked back along the riverbank. Neither of them spoke. When they reached the big iron gates of the foundry they stopped.

'Were you planning on marrying a solicitor?'

'I wasn't planning on marrying anybody.'

'Just as well with a tongue on you like that.'

She thumped him and he grabbed her and then kissed her very softly and then everything was all right again somehow.

'I missed you,' she told him.

The kiss was sweet. She had forgotten how it could be. He kissed her again and then he said, 'Can I see you on Saturday?'

'I have to help my mother with the shop—'

'Can't you take even half a day off? How about if I come to the bus station at about noon?'

'All right then,' she said. 'I do understand why you didn't want to go back to school and why you didn't want to stay in Sweet Wells. I cannot bear to look up the bank towards our house.'

Sep kissed her again, but briefly, and smiled at her before he left her at the foundry gates.

Eleven

Rose received Maddy's wages gratefully because takings were so far down at the shop that it no longer made a living. Mr Wilson had applied to the local builder and was extending his shop even more. She was irritated. Was he trying to take over the whole of the dale? She couldn't blame him for that, but the longer she was there the more she grew to dislike it.

She had hung on because at first they had no other income and nowhere else to go, and she had kept hanging on because she couldn't think what else to do, but now that Maddy was established at Black's and was getting a fair wage it was time to think of somewhere else to live.

One night when she had just locked up and gone upstairs she heard a banging on the door. She went downstairs. Most people came to the shop door but then few people came any more at all. Being widowed and poor, she had discovered, did not help you to make friends. It was Cuthbert Felix.

'Mrs Grant. Good evening.'

She asked him in and they went upstairs.

'I think we must talk about the shop.'

'I know we must,' she said.

'We must close it eventually. The competition is too good and we have not the room here to do what they are doing.'

'I agree. When will you want to close down?'

'Within the next few months.' He hesitated. 'I don't want to close it because I'm not sure how you'll manage without it, but I don't want you to think you have to stay here indefinitely.'

'We are managing, what with Maddy's job but I have

been glad of the shop.' She smiled at him. 'It gives me something to occupy my mind. I hope that doesn't sound too desperate. I'm not sure that we can afford to rent a house.'

'I may be able to help there. I own several cottages and one of them is bound to come up for rent soon.' He looked awkward suddenly. 'I just want you to know that I will not abandon you. I know the shop isn't making much money and I will let you have a cottage at a rent you can afford.'

'You're very kind to us. I don't want you to feel under an obligation,' Rose said. 'If you want to move somebody in here—'

'I don't. Mr and Mrs Wilson are enough to undermine anybody's confidence,' he said, smiling back at her. 'I just want you to know that you will have the first cottage which becomes vacant and until that time you are welcome to stay here and we will keep the shop open until then. I want you not to worry about any of it.'

'I won't,' Rose said.

When she let him out there was an awkwardness between them. There was no reason for him to be so good to them, but he seemed to want to be even though he was getting nothing out of it.

She was so grateful that she felt weak and it was only when he left that she leaned against the wall behind the back door and wanted to cry. She didn't because it was a stupid thing to do and Maddy had gone visiting the old ladies she used to work for. It was getting dark and she felt like sobbing, everything was so difficult. Why did things not get easier? Instead she went upstairs and put the kettle on to boil and soon she heard the sound of Maddy clashing the gate shut as she came through the yard.

Rose did not want to tell her that they had to move again, but she presumed Maddy would already know, it had become obvious over the past months. She would say nothing for now. Only when Mr Felix had a vacant cottage need anything be done and that might take some time.

* * *

Maddy's first meeting with Mr Black's son, David, happened quite soon. She knew the Blacks had two children, Iris who was just older than she was and David a little younger. She had met Mrs Black briefly. She came into the office occasionally but she looked Maddy up and down and merely said, 'Good morning. Is my husband here?'

'Oh, yes, of course,' Maddy had said and that was all.

They were not, she thought, going to be friends and the dreams she had had of being invited to the Black house, which she understood to be very grand, were shattered. She was the help. Iris, who was about her age, did not come to the office at all but David did and she liked him straight away.

He was very like his father, he had the same green eyes, the same friendly smile. It would be wonderful, her romantic nature told her, to fall in love with somebody like David, who would look after her, marry her, have children with her, provide for a family like so many men did.

He had a gentle air of confidence which Maddy thought she had not seen on anyone before. Perhaps if you were brought up to be Mr Black's son you would feel like that. She tried to talk to him.

'Will you be coming into the business then, to help your father?'

She was astonished when he laughed.

'Oh, no, I shouldn't think so. I'm going to join the Royal Navy. I love the sea.'

'Who will take over the business?' she asked and when he frowned she could see that he had not even thought about it, that it didn't matter to him and she thought that strange because his grandfather had started the business back before eighteen eighty and his father had built it up, carried it on.

She would have loved to have had something like that. It was one reason why she had always hankered after the house which was her home. It was part of who you were, part of who your family was.

'Oh, I expect my father will sell it,' he said breezily, but his eyes had clouded over and she knew that she had introduced him to a new concept.

David obviously had no idea that people did not go on for ever but then as far as she knew he had never lost anybody he cared about. His father was still there, working hard, solid and dependable. She wondered whether Mr Black knew that David did not care for steel founding, that he was working hard for nothing more than their day-to-day existence and general prosperity.

Maddy was however rather taken aback the day that she was asked to take some papers up to the house to Mrs Black. She didn't know what they were, something legal, and she presumed it was to do with the house. Mr Black had asked her casually to take them and as it was a short walk on a nice day she enjoyed it, but she was quite astonished when she got there and found how modestly they lived.

She had assumed they were rich people, they employed dozens of other people and must be making a good profit but the garden was unkempt, Mrs Black opened the door herself, and when Maddy was ushered into the hall she was amazed at how shabby it was in a comfortable unassuming way that she liked. She wasn't sure it would impress other people though.

She soon began to realize why the Blacks lived modestly. The nuns from the local convent came to the office, and Mr Black knew them well and they went off with a cheque. The people who ran the orphanage came and they went off with a cheque too. There were letters from local charities and nobody was refused.

Maddy was very proud of Mr Black for helping so many people in the area because there were a great many poor people in Durham and in the villages around the city and he would go with his wife at weekends to open leek shows and coffee mornings, whist drives and church bazaars.

How he talked her into it, Maddy wasn't quite sure because Mrs Black seemed to her anything but persuadable but she typed the letters so she knew what was going on. And every time he donated a silver cup or a money prize or gave a donation of some sort.

David went to university and the girl, Iris, had gone to

the local girls' grammar school and was now at the Royal Victoria Infirmary training to be a nurse. There weren't many families of their social standing who would have encouraged their daughter to do such a thing. Maddy was just grateful that Mr Black was so forward-thinking about women's education and social standing or he would not have given her the job in his office.

Mr Black's way of thinking was rare. To her it was an entirely new notion. The men that she had known before him were only concerned with making as much money as they could and spending it on themselves and their immediate families, not using it to help other people.

The first time that Sep and Maddy spent the day together in Durham it was a fine sunny afternoon. She wished that she had not lied to her mother, she had told her that Mr Black wanted her to go in and do some extra work that day and her mother could hardly object. They needed her pay so badly and her mother had not forgotten that sometimes if he kept her late Mr Black drove her home. He also paid Maddy what her mother thought was a good wage.

All the same, as the bus took her down the winding road and up on to the top where the little pit villages were on her way to Durham, Maddy could not help but feel guilty.

She could see Sep standing waiting for her because the bus was slightly late as it turned in to the bus station in North Road. She could not help comparing him somehow with David Black. Sep had the slightly unkempt air of somebody who lived alone, like a tall street urchin somehow with his hair in his eyes, as though there was no one to care for him, as indeed there wasn't.

She could see two girls looking at him as they went past though he didn't look up. He was very striking even in old clothes. He looked world-weary for somebody so young, leaning against the wall with his hands in his pockets and a cigarette between his lips.

David had a well-kept air and the confidence of somebody who came from a monied family and had never had to worry about anything. Sep had nothing other than an office job. He no longer looked like the solicitor's son. Until he opened his mouth he was just another Durham lad.

When she got off the bus, however, he smiled and was transformed. He threw down the cigarette, put his foot on it and came to her and he said, 'Maddy, I was beginning to think you weren't coming.'

His voice was as pure as the river at Wearhead and his manners were good. He held her arm as she got off the bus and took her away to a little tea shop in the winding Silver Street which led steeply towards the Market Place.

'The bus was late,' she said, kissing him decorously on the cheek so that he stopped as soon as there was a side street nearby so that he could kiss her properly.

Aware that he didn't have much money she was careful not to order anything that was dear and when they had eaten their Welsh rarebit and drunk their tea they set off down the steps beside Brown's Boathouse next to Elvet Bridge and ducked under the bridge and followed the towpath around the riverbanks under the shadows of the cathedral and up on to Palace Green. There they sat on a wooden bench and watched people walking to and from the cathedral.

'Where did you tell your mother you were?' he asked.

'I said I was working.'

'Why didn't you tell her you were seeing me?'

'She wouldn't approve.'

'And if there's a next time?'

Maddy didn't answer and then she said, 'I just wish you hadn't left, that's all.'

He didn't say anything to that and it occurred to Maddy for the first time that he might have left for more than because his father had hit him.

'Did you have somebody here in Durham?' she said.

He looked up very quickly and in his eyes there was astonishment.

'No.' He looked down again.

'You're lying to me. Was it a girl?'

'No, of course it wasn't.' He spoke quickly as though he was lying and wanted to be well beyond it, to have the subject be anything but this. 'Why would I want anybody else?'

'So you don't have anybody?'

He looked at her again, this time with impatience.

'If I had what the hell would I be doing buying you lunch when I can hardly afford to pay my rent?' he said.

'You didn't have to.'

'Maddy, look—'

'But you have somebody here?'

He hesitated and then he said definitely, 'I have no one here.'

'You can tell me the truth.'

There was another slight silence and then he said, 'My mother used to live here.'

Maddy stared at him.

'I thought she died when you were little.'

'No.' He held his breath, then exhaled sharply. 'She walked out so that she could live with another woman, and she never came back. I saw her and confronted her and they went away and . . .'

His voice trailed off. Maddy couldn't believe it.

'That's awful,' she said, 'but it shouldn't stop you from coming back. Maybe you miss home.'

'I don't miss it.'

'How did you know I was there?'

'I saw you when you were on the way to work weeks ago.'

'I wish that you would come back to the village,' she said.

'I shall never come back.'

Maddy spent moments taking this in and even then all she could think was that Mr Ward was not a very nice man so it was hardly surprising Sep's mother had left. She could not understand how any woman could leave a little boy and Sep must have been a very appealing little boy because small children always were; he would have been lovely, all dark eyes and black hair.

Maddy couldn't imagine a parent doing such a thing. Was Sep making this up to gain her sympathy?

'Your mother really lived with another woman?'

He nodded. Maddy didn't think it wise to pursue the subject.

'I must go.'

He walked her to the bus station.

'Next Saturday?' he asked as they stopped.

'I can't.'

'The one after then.'

'Sep—'

'Perhaps you're the one with somebody else?' he said.

She looked at him. 'What on earth do you mean?'

'I mean have you met someone in Durham?' His voice was like steel.

'Of course I haven't.' It was a ridiculous idea and made her smile and touch his hair and that was when he kissed her.

'The Saturday after next then?'

'All right,' she agreed.

He saw her on to the bus. She hated leaving him there, it didn't seem right to go back to the dale alone. When she finally got home she could see the lights on in his father's house and wanted to run in and tell his father that he was by himself in Durham, that he had nobody and nothing and . . . but she couldn't and if his father didn't want him there then there was nothing she could do about it.

She was almost home when she realized that he was right, she had met somebody in Durham. David Black. She liked him and she liked the way that the Blacks lived, there was something more sophisticated about it rather than the way that most people lived. They thought beyond themselves and their money, they had morals and principles.

Their family name meant something here in Durham; they were respected, well thought of. She had not known before now that that was something she had lost when her father died and the rest of the family had had to leave their home. They were nobody now and it mattered. She didn't think it should have but it did and it was to do with a sense of place, of rightness, of being among your own people.

She would have given a lot to get that back and the way

things were going it didn't seem likely that she would. The shop was taking nothing. Her mother stood behind the counter wearing a worried look on her face.

Suddenly Maddy felt the responsibility of looking after her as she had not before and she wished that her father was still alive or that someone would come forward and say 'Don't worry, Maddy, I'll take care of it' but nobody ever did.

Twelve

Sometimes Mr Black was not well and it looked as if David's dream to go to sea was long forgotten, if not by him then at least by his family. Nothing was said, nobody announced that when David was not away he would come into the office, but that first Christmas he came home he went straight into the office. His father protested, but only mildly because no doubt it was every father's dream to have his son come into the business.

David had no separate office and sat further along in the big office and it made her happy when he was there. She felt less responsibility for Mr Black and though it sounded silly when she thought of it Mr Black was more cheery when David was there. Though it might have been her imagination she thought the lines on his face were less defined after David came to the office during his holidays.

She felt slight sympathy for him because she thought many university students would spend their spare time doing what they wanted. It could not be said that the foundry was what David wanted and at first she thought he might have resented the implication that his future should be taken care of like that but he never let his mood show. He was always the same with her, always polite and sometimes funny, and she found that she was looking forward to his holidays even if he could not be.

The long summer days were the best, week upon week of good weather when she did not mind the bus journeys between the dale and the city because the days were so drawn out and sometimes on Saturdays she would go into town and see Sep though not often. She had no money and he had little and her mother was beginning to question the way that she appeared to be spending every day but Sundays at Black's Foundry and she found lying difficult.

The summer after David finished university his father would go home for his dinner at noon but David had asked for sandwiches because he said it was too nice to be indoors and since she had sandwiches too he suggested to her that they should walk through the town and sit on the river-banks. Almost every day they had a picnic.

'I saw you walking on Elvet Bridge last Saturday,' he said, one early September day.

'Oh?'

'You had a man with you. Tall and dark.'

'Sep Ward. He comes from my village. He lives in town now and we sometimes see one another on Saturdays.'

'A sweetheart then?' he said, his green eyes teasing.

She was about to disclaim, but she hesitated and thought she was no longer sure whether she cared about Sep or not. Her bond with Sep was very special, but she could not tell David about it and was feeling more and more guilty about seeing him while not telling her mother. She had a feeling that Rose would not be happy about the connection.

There was a knocking on his door. Sep couldn't understand it. Mrs Kennedy went out to do the shopping early on Saturday mornings. He pulled open the door and there stood Maddy looking dismayed as though she wished she hadn't come. He glanced back into the room. It had never looked so poor, though it was neat because he owned nothing.

'I thought we were meeting at the bus station,' he said.

'I was – I was early.'

'How did you get in?'

'A tall, thin man was going out and I explained and he let me inside.'

She came past him, looking around her.

'It's very tidy,' she said.

He thought back to his father's house, and to what seemed

now like utter luxury, the great big rooms, fires in the bedrooms in cold weather, the view beyond his window of the hills going up from the valley, the sheep cream dots in the lush grass and the grey stone walls snaking across. His view here was over a red-brick wall where there was a gap between the houses.

Mrs Kennedy's cooking wasn't like Mrs Herries' cooking. Mrs Kennedy was a widow who took in lodgers to survive and her meals, though adequate, consisted of small portions made with cheap meat and vegetables from the market. They ate lots of rabbit. He was sure it was good for you but full of very small bones and Mrs Kennedy cooked her vegetables to wilting.

Breakfast was always porridge. Sep had learned to hate porridge made with water and salt and without embellishments. The thought of Mrs Herries' bacon, eggs and fried bread on Saturdays could reduce him to misery. He no longer ate in the middle of the day because he had his rent to pay. He bought second-hand clothes from the covered-in market and had saved what was left to take Maddy out.

The day was bright, the window was open to the city sounds, somebody shouting in the distance and the bustle of the streets beyond the alleyway. The little room was stuffy.

He was only glad that Mrs Kennedy was big on washing and cleaning. He had hot water every morning and evening for himself. She shook her head over the worn clothes but she did scrub them and the little room wore a faint air of polish. Mrs Kennedy called it 'keeping the dirt at bay'. She did everything she could for her lodgers which cost nothing because she charged them quite a lot of money to stay there, but he knew it was better than some places having seen several before he reached this haven. In the evenings Mrs Kennedy played her piano in her room downstairs.

His landlady had only two rooms for herself: a bedroom and sitting room combined. The kitchen she also considered hers. The dining room at the front was for what she called 'her guests'. The piano was very out of tune and to make it worse she played 'Drink To Me Only With Thine Eyes' which reminded him so much of the old Grant house and Maddy that he would very often go for a walk unless it was pouring with rain or freezing, just to get out of the way.

Maddy sat down on the single bed. It creaked under her slight weight but there was nowhere else to sit and the room which had always seemed tiny to him was even smaller with somebody else in it. He saw her glancing around at the scarred wardrobe, the rickety chest of drawers.

'What's wrong?' he said.

'I don't think I should come here on Saturdays any more,' she said.

'You came all the way to my lodgings to tell me that?'

'It seemed fair.'

'And now that you've seen how poor I really am why should you bother.'

'It's nothing to do with that. I told my mother I was working. I don't think she believes me any more and it isn't fair to Mr Black to tell lies about it.'

'All right,' he said. 'Suit yourself.'

'It's not like that.'

Sep got up and held the door open for her and she started to cry. He thought maybe it was for show and she would stop, but she didn't and he closed the door and went back to her.

'Will you stop doing that?'

His pleas seemed to make the storm worse somehow. She put herself against his shoulder when he sat down and cried into his shirt.

'Look, Maddy, I'm not messing about here, I really care about you. I'm sorry if it doesn't suit your mother. I'm not exactly a brilliant catch any more and if you want not to see me I won't bother you, I won't come to the foundry and harass you or anything. Don't cry.'

He waited again for her to stop and when she lay there against his shoulder he put his arms around her but she drew away as though suddenly aware of the situation.

'I've got enough money to take you out for a splendid lunch,' he said.

'I don't need a splendid lunch.'

'I think we both do.'

She looked up at him and then she put her fingers on the back of his neck and drew him towards her and when he kissed her the little bed creaked in protest. Maddy drew away again and then she got up, smoothed her skirt, took off her hat but when he didn't move she sat back down again and kissed him and pushed him down and then stopped and looked into his eyes.

'You're very careful, aren't you?' she said.

'Oh, hell, yes. Every moment I think you're going to leave me.'

'I don't think I can. I don't think I remember how.'

A door slammed below.

'That's Mrs Kennedy coming back with exciting ingredients for supper. Rabbit stew, I suspect.'

They tiptoed down the stairs. Maddy stopped at the outside door. From the back of the house came strains of Mrs Kennedy playing the piano. Maddy flinched.

'Oh dear,' she said with a comical look at him. 'Let's get out of here,' and they did.

It was Monday morning, a fine morning not long after this meeting and Sep was working when he heard a noise just outside his office. He stopped writing and looked up. A tall dark man stood in the doorway. Sep got to his feet.

'Good morning. May I help you?'

The man looked quizzically at him and Sep thought he was not the usual kind of visitor. Visitors tended to be men from the shipyards come to look at the castings but not the owners. This man looked like an owner.

He was expensively dressed, quite out of place in the grubby little office, and had a proprietorial air, almost a swagger, which Sep could have resented had he had to put up with much of it. He didn't much like the way that the man looked at him, it was critical and his gaze went around the office as though things wouldn't quite do.

As they stood the manager must have heard the noise through the glass door and he came out, saying, 'Good morning. Do come in.'

Sep went back to his work. Mr Gregson shut the door and for a while their voices rose and fell. Then they came out and as they did so Sep felt very strange. There was something about the man which made him feel stupid and young and inadequate, something Mr Gregson had never made him feel. He didn't look up, but instead got on with what he was doing.

Once the man had left Mr Gregson said, 'Come in, Sep, and close the door.'

He went into the inner office. Mr Gregson was looking down at the desk as though something fascinating was happening there. He didn't say anything for so long that Sep grew bored and then with a sigh and a regretful look from under his eyebrows he said, 'I'm going to have to let you go.'

Sep looked at him but Mr Gregson didn't look at him again and Mr Gregson's face was red and his mouth was set as though he very much disliked what he had had to say.

'What, sack me?'

'I'm afraid so, yes.'

'Have I done something wrong?'

Mr Gregson shrugged for a moment or two and then he looked at him and Sep could see he was angry.

'No, lad, you haven't done anything wrong. You should get another job quite easily as you're good. It's just that Matthews will be coming back and there isn't enough work for both of you. You can finish the week.'

Sep knew instantly that this had nothing to do with Matthews as he had heard from the pitmen that Matthews had left Durham. He knew that Mr Gregson felt obliged to tell him a lie because he respected and liked him.

'Yes, of course. Thank you for giving me the chance in the first place,' Sep said, and went out.

He went back to his desk, thinking Mr Gregson wouldn't like him to go leaving things undone and he had a great deal of work to do if he was to finish everything before Friday. Then he looked up and saw his reflection in the glass and a very peculiar feeling came over him. The man had made him feel like his father made him feel, as though a disapproving voice would kick in at any minute and he remembered the man's voice because it had the faint uplift which everyone had in the dale.

He thought at first it was a mistake. He had never seen the man before so why should there be any connection, but the reflection in the glass told him otherwise and he was shocked. They looked alike.

He went on trying to do the wages. The figures blurred, moved. He wanted to make some excuse and yet he didn't so that he could think about this and then Mr Gregson came through to say he had to go down the pit.

'Do you want me to come with you?' Sep said, as though such an offer might mean he would not have to leave.

'No, I'll be fine. You just get on with the wages.'

Sep watched him go, sat still for a moment, and then began rifling through the filing cabinets in the inner office which he had never touched before and it was not long before he found what he was looking for. He had known that the pit did not belong to Mr Gregson. It was a very small part of the Embleton Mining Company.

The Embleton Mining Company was based in Northumberland, run out of Alnwick, had huge pits on the coast and lots of tiny little ones like this in different areas. Eventually he unearthed more information on the company. The man who owned it was called Ward. Jonas B. Ward. B for bastard, Sep could not help thinking.

He turned around. Mr Gregson was standing in the doorway.

'You aren't supposed to come in here when I'm not here,' he pointed out.

Sep hesitated and then thought he might as well go on since he had so obviously jeopardized the wages they owed him. Did it really matter now?

'Who is he?'

'He's the owner. It isn't anything for you to worry about.'

'He made you get rid of me. He wouldn't have done that without a good reason.'

'He didn't like the look of you.'

'I didn't like the look of him either.'

'You'll get another job easily enough.'

'I was happy with this one and he had no right to put me out of it when I hadn't done anything.'

'It wasn't what you did, lad—'

'No, it's quite obviously who I am. Who is he?'

Mr Gregson hesitated.

'I can't tell you anything about it. All I know is that he's my employer and I have to do what he wants if I am to keep my own job. I'm sorry, Sep, I really am. I don't want to lose you. You're honest and capable and you have a future in this business if you want it but not here apparently. Try not to let it get to you. I'll give you a decent reference.'

'That's kind of you, but first I have to go to Northumberland and sort this out.'

'I wouldn't do that, he has a reputation as a hard man and you're hardly more than a boy. It won't do you any good to confront him and I'll make sure you get taken on in another pit office. There's plenty of them.'

'Thanks, Mr Gregson, but if I've already lost my job I've got nothing to lose by going to see him, have I?'

Mr Gregson said nothing but shook his head.

'Look,' he said eventually, 'he's a man of tremendous influence. If he chose you would never get another job in mining within a hundred miles of here. Leave it alone, that's my advice.'

Sep put down the papers and he got up and walked out, collecting his coat as he went and slamming the door after him.

It was dark when Sep got off the train because although it was almost summer the rain had set in hard with a wind behind it. There was nothing to tell him in that darkness where Jonas Ward lived but he followed the street until he met someone and all he said was where was Ward's house and he was directed by a pointing finger until the small town came to an end and there were big iron gates and a long winding drive and he could hear the sea getting nearer and then he came to the house. It was massive, the biggest house he had ever seen with great tall chimneys reaching up in the sky and the sound of the sea not far beyond. He banged like hell on the front door and eventually it was opened by a pretty woman who peered up at him.

'Mr Ward at home? I'd like to see him. I'm Sep Ward.'

She let him in because she was startled at the name, he presumed, and once in the big wide wooden panelled hall which had a wrought-iron dog-leg staircase reaching high up into the top of the house he just followed the line of light and pushed open the door.

The man he had seen earlier that day was standing by the fire as though he hadn't been home long and was ready for his dinner. He had a glass in his hand. He had been facing the fire because it was the kind of night for sitting over one but turned at the noise.

'So, what did you do that for?' Sep said.

He stared for a moment or two and then seemed to recover fairly quickly.

'Mary!' he bellowed, 'who the hell are you letting in?'

The woman appeared in the doorway. She didn't look like a servant, she was far too expensively dressed for that, Sep thought, and she didn't act like one either. She merely looked at him and then went out and closed the door. Nobody spoke.

'You didn't have to put me out of my job,' Sep said. 'I needed it.'

'Get out,' the man said, turning back to the fire.

'I'm not going anywhere until you tell me why you did that.'

There was a long pause and it ended when the man turned around again.

'I can have you thrown out.'

'I was good at it. If I hadn't been I would have accepted your decision, but I'm good at my job.'

'You'll get another.'

'I was quite happy with that one and I need the money.'

'Yes, you look as if you do,' Jonas said, regarding Sep's shabby suit with some distaste. 'Why don't you get out?'

'I'm not going anywhere until you give me an explanation.'

'Who told you that you could come here?'

Sep didn't answer that.

'And how did you find me?'

'I looked through the filing. It wasn't exactly difficult.'

'Go back to Durham,' Jonas said.

Sep stood where he was and held the other man's gaze until he turned back to the fire.

Jonas said softly, 'Did you quarrel with your father?'

'Did you?'

'I don't want you anywhere near my business. You had no right to come here.'

'You put me out because of who I am and that isn't right. You don't know me. If you'd hung around in the dale long enough you might have done, but you don't so it was unjust.' Sep could hear his voice. He was shouting. He was so angry. It was stupid, he knew it was. He could not intimidate this man by yelling at him but somehow he couldn't help it. 'I was no threat and Mr Gregson and I got on really well. You embarrassed him, you made him look and feel small and there was no need.'

'You knew who I was, or you would have worked it out, clever as you are,' Jonas said.

'I didn't even know your name, I hadn't thought about who owned the place and the Embleton Mining Company doesn't exactly give it away, but we look alike. I could see it as soon as you had gone when I saw myself in the mirror and you made me feel like my father used to. How related are we?'

'I'm your father's brother.'

'I thought you must be. And is that why you don't want me there?'

Jonas didn't answer.

'I don't like the connection,' he said.

'The connection is with your brother who presumably you don't like. It's nothing to do with me.'

'You're right, it was unjust, but I want nothing more to do with any family from that place.'

'I don't live there. I live in Durham.'

'I guessed you'd left the dale. Your father would never have let you become a clerk in such a place. Didn't you go to school? Didn't you have real ambitions?'

'I still have real ambitions,' Sep said. 'I'm going to be a mine manager.'

'You like mining?' He was curious, Sep could see, and his eyes were warmer than they had been.

'Some people do. You obviously do or you wouldn't have made it your life's work.'

'I was a solicitor, like your father, I specialized in crime. I was very fond of my profession and then I left and . . . once I got away, once I wasn't anything to do with my family I thought I'd really been doing that to please my father and grandfather and that I might go into business.

'I met a man who was a pit sinker and we got on like brothers – not like the brother I had, not like your father, but like people think of brothers when they never are. He was good at his job and I liked being my own boss and the whole idea of bringing up from the earth something as vital as coal and not having anybody tell me what to do and not having any responsibilities . . . well, it had appeal.

'I stuck with it and we started to make money and I've made money ever since. I turned out to be a good businessman and a good miner. Some people are born to do certain things. They don't know why but they are.'

Sep didn't like to say anything but the things Jonas was saying made him want to run back to the office and start again.

'That's how I feel about it.'

'You don't have sufficient experience to know yet.'

'I knew the minute I walked in the door of the pit office.'

'Have you been underground?'

'I don't know why everybody makes such a fuss of it.'

'Because one day you might need to go down there to save somebody's life or you might need somebody to save yours.'

'I know all that.'

Jonas said nothing and Sep felt as though he should go but he couldn't, not until he had made his point.

'You've got no reason to get rid of me. I'm not in contact with my father or anybody in the dale I would talk to about you. I'm just another lad in Durham trying to make enough money to get by on for now. Mr Gregson thinks I'm good, or at least he says he does.'

Still Jonas said nothing. Sep couldn't think of anything more that would help. Finally Jonas stopped studying whatever he had been gazing at so intently and looked at Sep.

'Give me my job back. I'll work twice as hard and I'll pretend we aren't related at all. I don't care about you or your money or how . . . powerful you are. Things like that don't matter to me. I just want to be there.'

Jonas was silent for another moment or two and then he looked straight at Sep. 'Why don't you stay the night? Have some supper with us. You can go back to Durham in the morning and I'll tell Gregson to give you your job back.'

'He'll think I'm stupid.' Having got what he wanted Sep was so surprised he couldn't think what to say.

'No, he won't.'

'Well, he'll think you're stupid.'

'He already knows that.'

'You don't have to give me anything,' Sep said. 'I'm happy to work for what I need.'

'Don't worry, I'm not going to.'

Jonas was right. The meal was superb: home-made vegetable soup, roast beef, chocolate pudding. Mary sat with them and two other women served the dinner and took the dishes away.

'Do you eat like this every night?' Sep asked as they sat back at the end of it. Mary had gone off without a word with her coffee.

'Yes.' Jonas considered the port in his glass and the Stilton in front of him. 'I like food and wine and I work hard so . . . How's your father?'

'I haven't seen him lately.'

'You don't get on?'

'Maybe sons never get on with their fathers.'

'He was always a mean bastard.'

'He is.'

The moment he had said it Sep wished he hadn't. He had never said such a thing to anyone but Maddy. Why should he say it in front of Jonas?

'He certainly was when I knew him.'

'My mother left.'

'It was difficult for her,' Jonas said.

'Being married and having a child?'

Did Jonas know what had happened? Sep wasn't sure, his uncle's face was one of the most unreadable he had ever come across.

'Women get married. It's what they do, most of them. We haven't given them a lot of choice.'

'Do you know why she left?'

Jonas looked coolly at him.

'I think she left him because he was impossible.'

'She went off with another woman. Did you know that?'

'How brave of her.'

'I didn't think it was brave. I thought it was just the opposite.'

'Of course you did because she left you. If she'd been your father and left it wouldn't have looked quite so bad.'

'It wouldn't have felt any bloody different,' Sep said. 'Mind you, I don't think I would have cared if he'd gone just as long as there was enough money to get by on.'

'Ah, there lies the problem. What is enough? You haven't forgiven her?'

'I shall never forgive her.'

Jonas sighed. 'We're such grudge bearers in our family. My God, we're good. Have some port.'

Sep did. He couldn't help gulping it down.

'I saw her,' he said after the first sweet mouthful. 'She lived in Durham all the time and she never once tried to see me.'

'Maybe she did want to see you. Maybe she thought her way of life would be disgusting to you.'

'It was.'

'You think she should have stayed?'

'No, I think she should have taken me with her.'

'Your father was a lawyer. Do you think he would have allowed it?'

'He didn't want me. What difference did it make?' Somehow Sep could hear his cry echo all over the room. 'When I found her after ten years she ran away again and not from him. She ran from me. She still didn't want me. Neither of them . . .' He stopped then because he ran out of controllable breath. And he wished he hadn't had anything to drink, was cursing himself because he wouldn't have blurted all that out when he was sober and never to somebody like Jonas who was obviously as hard as hell and didn't give a damn about anybody.

'I'm sorry, I didn't mean to say all that. I think I'd better go.'

'Not now. It's late and it's dark. You can go in the morning.'

Sep said nothing. He didn't really want to go anywhere, he was tired suddenly, it had been a very long day.

'You really liked working at the pit in Durham?'

'Yes, I really did.'

'Gregson said you were good. Do you want to go to bed?'

'Yes.'

Mary showed him into a huge bedroom with a roaring

fire, a big bed and acres of carpet. The heavy curtains were pulled across the windows. He thanked her and when she had gone he pulled off his clothes and crawled into bed and slept.

Thirteen

It was a pretty little stone house, an end terrace, and once again it was smaller than her childhood home they had left. In some ways Maddy was loath to leave the shop since it gave her mother some kind of life and she couldn't think what else her mother might do so the full responsibility fell on her to earn a living for them.

She thought that Mr Black paid her well for what she did, but keeping them on her wage alone meant being careful with their money though they were used to that. They did not need to go far. Her mother was good at remaking clothes and they bought cheap material from the local market. There were shoes to buy but they didn't walk far so these lasted and her mother had long since learned how to make cheap nourishing meals.

At work Maddy had always been vague about her family and never said she was an only child, instead she made up a family for herself. She knew it was silly, but she had never liked being an only child so she talked of 'my sisters'. It was a small deception and brought her some comfort since she had nobody but her mother for family.

The house was set back from the road only a few inches. Inside there was a tiny lobby before you stepped into the kitchen which overlooked the yard. It had nothing in it but a coalhouse, a lavatory and a tiny grass path. Maddy had missed the garden since she had left their house on the tops.

She hoped that some day she might have a garden again. There was nowhere to sit outside in the summer; they could go and sit on the riverbank which was pleasant because the River Wear ran shallow through the village and the banks around it were perfect for picnics, but that had to be organized and it was not quite the same.

The stairs went up the middle of the house and were straight and narrow. To the other side was the sitting room, tiny with one window that looked out across the street. At the top of the stairs was a window facing out to the back of the cottage with a view of the hills rising up away from the village, on the other side of the valley from their house. Up there were two bedrooms. Enough for them.

Downstairs there was the range in the kitchen and a fire in the sitting room. That was all but as far as Maddy was concerned, who viewed it all with regard to her finances, it was quite big enough.

There was no sign on that Monday morning several weeks later that it was to be anything other than an ordinary day.

Sep was trying to forget this and concentrate on work mid-morning when he saw a shadow move. He looked up and there was Jonas. He was surprised and then worried. Jonas didn't look anything like his usual surly self, he looked serene, that was the only word for it. He got to his feet, trembling, and wondered whether he had done anything wrong lately. Mr Gregson had said he was pleased with him, that he should study and think about pit management.

'Good morning . . . sir,' Sep managed.

Jonas grinned.

'Hello, Sep. How are you?' he said easily.

Astonished, Sep gaped. Mr Gregson came out of the inner office and he was smiling too, though not as much as his employer, as though he had some idea of what was going on. He panicked. Had he done something this time? Was Jonas going to sack him again, but if so then he wouldn't be so friendly, surely?

'May we use your office, Gregson?' Jonas said.

Gregson nodded and went out.

'Come in here,' Jonas said, ushering him into Mr Gregson's for once unnaturally tidy office.

Jonas closed the door.

'How are you?' he said again.

Frustrated now, not knowing whether to stand or sit or what to say or do, Sep said, 'I'm fine.'

'Good. Look . . . have you had any contact with your father?'

'No, and I'm not going back and you can't make me and . . . I'll leave here if you make me.'

'I'm not going to make you do anything. Calm down and sit down, for goodness' sake, you're making me nervous.'

Sep waited, but Jonas obviously wasn't going to go on until he had sat down so he did.

'Mr Gregson says you have a great deal of ability, that you could do better things.'

'I don't want to do better things,' Sep said, not understanding. 'I was going to study law until everything went wrong, and then . . .'

'And then?'

Sep raised his eyes. Mr Gregson's big wall clock struck eleven and they listened to it until it stopped.

'I was going to do law to try and please my father when nothing I had done before that had pleased him. Getting good marks at school, he never mentioned them. When I was captain of cricket he never came to watch. He just went on every day as though I was invisible except that sometimes . . .'

'Except that sometimes he hit you.'

Sep stared at him. He wanted to deny it, wished he could, but he couldn't.

'How did you know?' he asked softly.

'He used to hit me. He hated anybody being as clever as he was. He really hated people who were cleverer than he was and that's both you and me.'

'But he tried to get me to go on and do my last year at school so that I could study law.'

'Perhaps that was for respectability's sake. He was always concerned about such things and he liked the stifling little society which exists in Sweet Wells.'

There was a short silence into which Sep finally managed, 'There's nothing wrong with the place.'

'I like that you defend it.'

'You're not going to sack me again, are you?'

'What would you do if I did?'

'Find another job at another pit, study to be a manager.' Jonas smiled and Sep felt bolder. 'You've smiled twice since you came in. Are you feeling all right?'

And that made Jonas laugh.

'I want you to come back to Northumberland and work for me,' he said.

Sep hesitated. Jonas waited and then he said, 'Have I got this wrong? You don't want to?'

'No, you haven't got it wrong, but I have . . . connections here.'

'Connections?'

'There is a girl.'

Jonas raised his eyebrows.

'A girl?'

'I love her.'

'Of course you do. What is she, a barmaid?'

'It's not like that. I want to marry her.'

'Dear God,' Jonas said and sat down.

Sep had such a wonderful thing to tell Maddy, he had not been able to keep his mind on work since Jonas had come to see him. He wanted to tell her how much things were going to change. He would make all their fortunes, he felt clever for the first time in his life, like he was in control, Jonas as magician, as deliverer.

'I've been offered another job, a better job,' he said, stumbling over the words in his haste to tell her.

'Really?' she said.

It was autumn in Durham, one of the best times of the year, he thought in glee. What better time to leave it and go to Northumberland where the grey water would be crashing over the rocks in the big October tides. He and Maddy would be settled in before Christmas.

She would get on with Mary, he thought, because she was a kind woman and he knew Maddy would love the big house. It would be like a dream come true for her, not back to her own house, but forward to something just as good. She wouldn't have to work if she didn't want to and Jonas would pay him well and he would buy her beautiful dresses.

They could be married and her mother could come to Northumberland with them and . . .

He was dying to tell her everything and yet was savouring the excitement before he did so.

They were sitting in a little tea shop on Palace Green and the cathedral was shadowed now because the day was dark.

Sep fidgeted.

'Will you come with me?'

Maddy looked at him. He looked down. He had said the same thing to her when he had left Sweet Wells. Was she remembering that?

'It isn't here,' he said. 'It's the top end of Northumberland. I'm asking you to marry me. I love you. I've always loved you. Will you marry me and come with me?'

Maddy couldn't answer him. She did love him. She wanted to be with him, wake up with him, hold him in her arms, be free to touch him. She wanted a house, children.

'That's lovely, Sep.'

'Is it?' He hesitated. 'But you aren't saying yes.'

'I have to think about my mother.'

'I know you do. Would your mother leave the dale?'

'She doesn't have a lot to stay there for.'

'We could all go. It's beautiful. Though the pits aren't, of course.'

'Is it another pit office?'

'My uncle Jonas owns the colliery there and he has a fine house and we would live with him and you'll love it, Maddy, it's right by the sea—'

'Your uncle?'

'He's offered me a good wage and in time I'll do better, once I go for my management qualifications. It's a new beginning, Maddy, a fresh start for us.'

Maddy took her mind back to leaving her home, her mother telling her that Jonas Ward was putting them out. She barely heard what Sep said after that, he was telling about how they had met, how Jonas owned the colliery where he worked in Durham and many others, how he had prospered almost from nothing, how Jonas had not wanted him there at all, but he had followed him to Northumberland.

He sounded so excited, she hadn't seem him like this before, his eyes were lit with happiness and he didn't stop talking until he needed breath which was most unlike him.

She gave him a moment or two to recover and then she said, 'I can't. I'm sorry, but I can't.'

That stopped him. He stared at her as though he had expected to hear her say something quite different which he had of course, and as though it took him time to understand that she was not saying what he had been certain she would.

'Why not?' he said finally and the light died away from his face and she was sorry that it had been such a temporary intrusion.

She didn't answer him, didn't know what to say. She couldn't tell him what had happened, her mother had made her promise not to and she had told her mother so many lies over the past months while she had been seeing Sep and more and more regularly.

Her mother trusted her completely. Sometimes it made her feel sick and her mother would not want her going around with him. Lately somehow the kisses had become harder and more important and she had longed to be alone with him. She was only glad that they did not go back to his lodgings as she wanted to be near. She longed to go to bed with him. It made her face burn to think of it but she wanted to pull his clothes off and have him pull her clothes off and to be as close as they could be.

'No,' she said.

'I know you think it isn't as good as being a solicitor—'

'It hasn't anything to do with that.'

'Hasn't it?'

'No, it hasn't.'

His eyes were hard now and unforgiving. She could see that he was not reassured.

'You always cared about these things. I will make my way and although we might not have any . . . any of that daft kind of middle-class status it will be a good life for us. Anyway, what am I saying? Jonas is a rich important man there. We'll have more status than anybody ever had in a stupid little dales village if you care for such things so much.'

'I don't care.'

'No? Then what?'

'I cannot explain.'

'You have to explain.'

She put down some coins on the table whereas normally he would pay and she ran out. She could see him getting to his feet with a hurt uncomprehending look on his face.

'Maddy, wait!' He was hampered by having to pay the rest of the bill.

She ran out of the café and across the green and down the narrow, steep path which led towards the riverbank.

She could hear him shouting her name as she reached the towpath and then she went across Prebends Bridge and disappeared among the trees. The leaves had turned lime and orange and she was aware that if she went to the bus station he would follow her. She knew that no matter how long she waited he would be there when she reached it so she made her way out of the city through the smaller streets until she reached a bus stop where she could catch a bus in the right direction.

The bus was a long time in coming and she had an hour or so to reflect on what she had said and on what she had not said. She could never explain to Sep what Jonas had done to them. Nobody knew that he owned their house, at least his brother knew and her mother but Sep obviously had no idea or he would not have suggested such a thing.

No, she thought, it was better to keep him ignorant than explain. The shame of it all would be too much for her mother to bear and her mother still hated Jonas for what he had done. She hated him too and would never do anything which would involve her with him.

Sep must have a good relationship with his uncle – he was obviously the only member of his family to have this and she would not change that. She could not ask him to choose between her and his uncle. That way he would not get the job he wanted. There was no other way in which they could be married, she knew it. She could not leave her mother in the dale, he would not come back to Sweet Wells and they had no money between them.

Sep wasn't going to leave it there. He spent all night sitting on his bed fuming, left the house as soon as it was light, and was standing outside her office that morning when she arrived, leaning against the wall beside the gate, his hands in his pockets. Worse still it was raining and he had no coat. He huddled there in against the wall as far as he could.

She had half thought he would be there, just as she had half thought he would turn up in Sweet Wells at her house the previous evening. She stopped, tried not to believe he was standing there, wondered whether if she closed her eyes he would disappear, that maybe it was just a nightmare and she would wake up in bed at any second. When none of these things happened she went wearily to him as she had to go past him to get into her office and he was more or less barring the door.

'What are you doing here?' she said.

'I don't think you understood me yesterday,' he said.

Maddy tried to answer him equably.

'I understood you perfectly. I cannot marry you, I cannot go with you. There's nothing more to be said.'

'I want an explanation.'

'I have work to do.'

She would have gone past him. Sep grabbed her arm and, obliged to stop, she turned around.

'Don't do that!' she said.

She stood while he let go of her. Various foundry men were walking past, some of them quietly, some of them staring, one of two eyeing the couple but talking to cover the scene.

'I'm not going anywhere with you. Is that clear enough?'

She was oblivious to other people and was almost shouting

and trying not to, trying to stay calm, she hated the idea of having a scene in a public place and was trying in vain to whisper.

'I want you to tell me why not,' he insisted.

He didn't say anything more, but she seemed to have to make it even clearer.

'I don't love you, I don't want you. Now go away and leave me alone!'

He stood like somebody who would like to leave but was so upset that he couldn't remember the way out of the gates even though it was only a few yards.

'I don't believe that.'

Maddy gritted her teeth and through them she said, 'I'm not going anywhere with you, not now and not ever. Surely that's clear enough even for you?'

She didn't intend to be cruel and hated the way they were doing this in public. All she could think was that if she could get rid of him and gain the security of the office that everything would be a lot better.

'Go away,' she said softly, watching the flood of workmen as they moved past.

'You seemed to like me well enough until I got this new job,' he protested.

She hesitated. She almost told him and then she felt that she couldn't because if she told him he wouldn't go and she cared enough about him to wish that he had a good relationship with his uncle, somebody like a parent who would look after him. Without his uncle's help, without experience, she had the feeling it would be a long time before he got anywhere because he had nobody to help and no connections or contacts. Men needed influence like that to get anywhere in life. And he had been so happy when he was telling her before she had turned him down.

'I don't want to go anywhere with you. I've been trying to end this for months, you know it.'

He said nothing, but looked down, beginning to waver. Perhaps overnight he had realized there was nothing he could do or say, she thought, and this was just one last-ditch attempt.

She could see that one or two of the foundry men were grinning. Her face burned. She half turned and glared at them. This was none of their business and it was not a spectacle for them. They shuffled away.

'I don't want anything more to do with you,' she said. 'Now, for the last time leave me alone.' Somehow she managed to put her key into the door of the office, and when she turned it the door almost miraculously opened, and she went blindly inside, closed the door and stood against it for a few seconds, breathing very heavily as though she had run a long way.

By herself in the office Maddy started to cry. Mr Black must be in the works, thank goodness. There was a noise in the doorway from the little office. She turned away when she heard it.

'Maddy?'

It was David Black. He didn't come into the office, he hesitated there as if unsure. Presumably he had seen and heard what had happened though she had not noticed him at the time. Maybe he had even come out of the office. Oh, horrors! She was ashamed, her face burned.

'Are you all right? Was that fellow bothering you?'

That fellow. Like Sep was somebody she didn't know, somebody unimportant. She thought of his shabby clothes and the way that he hadn't raised his eyes – it must look like that to David.

'It was nothing,' she said.

'I can go and see that he's off the premises.'

'No, no, I'm sure he's gone.'

Embarrassed now she wasn't sure how much David had heard, not much apparently if he thought Sep was just bothering her. He obviously didn't think it was the same young man he had seen her with before, the boy from home she had cared about so much. The tears receded. She turned to him. David's concerned green eyes were gentle. He came over.

'Sit down and I'll make you some tea.'

The offer was too good to resist. He made the tea and they drank it together.

'I should get on,' she said.

'Oh, don't worry. The old man's in the works and will be there for a while, I'm sure.'

She laughed. She quite liked hearing him speak so lightly and disrespectfully of the father whom she knew he adored. He knew how hard she worked, how much this place and everything in it mattered to her. She could not help comparing the two young men. Sep could have been like this. He could have been coming back telling her all that he was doing, helping his father in the Durham office. He could have had a future. Instead of which he had thrown it away and for what?

She was so angry with him that it was not until she was on the bus going home that evening that she remembered the things she had said to him and felt guilty. They were not true of course, she had always loved him.

It was the idea of Jonas Ward and the hateful things he had done to her family and even if Sep knew it would not alter things. He had chosen his path and she had chosen hers and they went in quite different directions.

She would learn to live without him. He could not break her heart. She thought of David, his lovely voice, his educated accent, his respected family and the way that they had sat down and drunk tea together. David was lovely.

'It was the boy from home,' he guessed once they had drunk their tea.

'Yes.' She wished David had not realized. It made things worse somehow.

'Not just anybody,' David encouraged her. 'You must have been seeing him for quite a long time.'

I've known him most of my life, Maddy thought, wanting to cry again.

'I broke it off. It wasn't right for me. He'll find somebody else. Now, we really must get on and do some work or your dad won't be happy when the orders don't get out.' She smiled at him and got up and began her typing.

She was so glad of the work. When there was nothing else it was always there, reassuring, comforting. It would take her mind off Sep and his awful uncle and the way that she would go back home tonight and pretend everything was all right. She could not say anything to her mother or her mother would worry.

Somehow they had switched places, it was if she were the parent and her mother was the child. She wished she had somebody she could confide in but there was no one. Normally she told Sep everything. Perhaps she would not be able to do that any more. She might never see him again. She tried not to panic, she had done the right thing but it didn't feel like that. She felt lonelier now than she had ever felt.

Mr Black's health wasn't very good the following winter. Sometimes he would take a funny turn in the office and go into his own little room and sit down. He did not say anything about this but Maddy had learned to look for the signs: paleness of face, shaking hands, slight confusion. Once or twice Mrs Black rang and said he could not come into the office and Maddy guiltily enjoyed these times because she got David to herself.

He was very quick, she thought admiringly. You never had to tell David anything twice and sometimes she would get halfway through an explanation and not need to go on because she would see the comprehension dawn in his eyes.

He knew the men. She suspected he had known them from being a little boy, that he had come to the office as a child. He was so much at home there that it hurt her to see how restless he could become.

At first he would gaze at the door as though he might make a getaway but the summer that his father had flu and was gone for almost six weeks David became totally engrossed in the business and that was when he changed and stopped thinking about doing something else with his life, and she could see how much he began to enjoy it and then to love it.

She saw him talking and smiling with the chemist and with various visitors to the office. His confidence grew. She could hear the strength in his voice when he answered the telephone. He knew which orders were at which stage.

He was good at dealing with the customers, but she had seen him taking charge in the works too. Some of the men were his father's age and liked his youth and enthusiasm and they trusted him, she could see by their banter and smiles. Others he had known as boys. He could pull the foundry together so that it worked as one unit and she admired his ability. Her perfect day was when she and David worked, often in silence, in the office together. She did not miss Sep, she told herself, she had David's company now.

Sometimes she dreamed that David would come into the office one day and ask her to a family gathering or to go for a drink. Sometimes her dreams took her further, that they would be together, that he would ask her to marry him and she would become part of the Black family, accepted into a set of people whom everybody respected.

Her mother would have been so proud. Maddy knew that her mother was quite desperate for her to marry a man of money and influence just as all mothers were, but then she knew her mother would have also been happy for her to marry any decent man whom she loved.

Sep was glad to go. He would put everything behind him. He would never think about Maddy and Sweet Wells again. It was finished, it was over and he didn't care.

In the days that followed Sep found out how mining worked on a big scale and he still loved it even though it was a dangerous profession and the men who did it were another breed: comradely towards one another, distrustful of outsiders, resident in almost closed communities, brave but not foolhardy in the main, respectful of one another, hard working because the more coal they turned out the more money they made.

His curiosity and desire to learn seemed to take his fears away and he liked the men, he admired their work and wanted to be part of it. He liked sitting in the pit office talking to Jonas and trying to sound intelligent even from the first when he had so little idea what the hell he was talking about. This was a much bigger operation than the little pit in Durham. Thousands of men worked here and it was complicated but he learned to love the intricacy of it all.

He liked being able to go back to Jonas's house in the evenings and eat a good dinner, sleep in a comfortable bed. It made up to a certain extent for his having had to leave Maddy and Durham behind him. He resolved never to think of her again. He would find somebody else and he felt right here as he had felt nowhere else in his life. Sweet Wells had never been like this. He felt as though he had come home.

Jonas gave him a few days and then when they were in the office together at the end of the day and ready to go home he said, 'What happened to the girl?'

'Nothing, I just misjudged it, that's all,' Sep said. 'She didn't want to marry me after all and I don't think I really wanted to marry her.'

'Women aren't all like that, you know.'

'Like what?'

'Like your mother and whatever the girl is called. Don't take against them.'

'Mary seems all right,' Sep said gruffly.

'Yes, she is,' Jonas said. 'You'll find somebody else.'

'I don't care right now. I'm happy to be here and I'll work hard and make something good here.'

'I'm sure you will,' Jonas said.

Fourteen

Cuthbert did not want to leave the dale. He had got to the stage where he didn't want to leave his house. He was going quietly mad from having nobody to talk to and had taken to gardening and even cooking to stave off the boredom.

It was not so bad when the rain, snow, wind or hail kept him at home but when the nights grew lighter he could not bear his own company and the sight of other people socializing. He was sure everybody else had friends, yet he did not know how to do more than pass people in the street and nod. He tried smiling and saying hello, but people were not used to him doing so and they looked through him.

And although he went for long walks in the fine weather people were not open to conversation, it had taken him too long to attempt it. He was always going to go to concerts in the church or chapel at Stanhope or join some kind of meeting or society but he could not go. He could not get himself out of the house. He would brood upon the idea all day and then tell himself that he had changed his mind. He felt so much better for not going, he preferred the silence of his house.

The trouble was also that on the odd occasion that he did get into conversation he was bored. He waited for the other person to stop talking so that he could hear what his voice sounded like. If anybody came to the house he became unhappy until they left. He grew used to his loneliness.

From the spring of 1939 he watched Hitler's progress and could soon tell that there would be a war. He was a young man, he was fit, he would be called upon to fight and he began to think about it. He could not imagine what it was like to have to go and fight against a common enemy. He had never had to face anything of the kind. The trouble was, he thought now, letting the memories flood back, that his father had died in the trenches of the First World War in France and his mother had never stopped mourning him and in a sense waiting for him to come back. There had been nobody else in her life, she had hated war because of it and he found that he was feeling sick at the idea.

Once he thought about having to leave his secure home in the dale the terrors came upon him and he could not think about anything else. It became easier to go and offer himself to the army instead of waiting for them to come to him.

He knew that he was not officer material. He could not tell anybody to do anything and had no idea how to lead. He was too much of a loner to do anything like that, so gave himself up to the notion of having to fight. Although he lay in bed sweating and worrying he knew that other men would be called to do the same and though he thought himself totally unfitted for such a thing – how did you ever kill another man, it made him shudder just to think of it? – he would not hide there in the dale, playing the coward.

He knew that if it came to a war he would die. Dying was not something he could contemplate with any degree of equanimity and neither did he think he could let other men do his fighting for him. If he had never done a fair thing in his life he must tackle it now.

He went to the nearest recruiting station and joined up to be a common soldier.

By the late summer of 1939 it had become obvious that men would be needed to fight a war and by September, when war had been declared, Sep was fired up to go and fight for his country.

He had tried talking to Jonas at home but he would not listen and now he had tried talking to him on a short wet September evening in the privacy of his office at the biggest of his pits and he still wasn't listening. Sep was beginning to think he never would. Jonas was not the most patient of men and he regarded Sep like he would have regarded an idiot.

'This is not a tuppence ha'penny operation we're running here. I can't run it without managers.'

'You could get other managers,' Sep said. 'There are plenty of competent men . . .'

Sep stopped. Jonas had looked up from the desk and was eyeing him with a look Sep had come to know well.

'I shouldn't have to tell you how important the work is. The whole of the war rests on coal. The factories need to produce the necessary weapons, for the steel foundries to provide the ships. A lot of the pitmen will be going to war, yes, but with all due respect to them they can be replaced though whether they should be is another matter. It's going to be bad enough managing with the reduced work force we will have.

'We will lose a great many young men and as you know only too well the work we do is demanding, difficult and dangerous. I need you here no matter what stupid ideas you have that you will be better off being shot at in France. Any bugger can do that too.' He paused. 'Your work is vital and only you are able to do it. I wish I could do everything by myself, I know you are so keen to go away and die heroically for your country, but you aren't going so you might as well forget about it.'

'It isn't that I want to go and get shot at—'

'Isn't it? What then, you think you could fly an aeroplane, you want to join the navy, what? You think you'd be better at that than doing your job, something you've been trained to do and God help us are good at?'

Sep couldn't think.

'I just want to help.'

'You are helping. You won't be allowed to go. Go and do it. I don't want anybody to hear you complaining.'

Sep left the office thinking about how lucky he was. He lived in the huge house where he was so well looked after he had occasional guilt feelings about it as though he had no right to any of it. He earned a wage as good as any solicitor and probably more than most.

He knew also that many of the mines paid their men badly, that owners would not provide up-to-date methods so that the men were often absent and resented the way that things were done. Nationalization would for the greater part be a good thing but it was not the way things were done here. Jonas would never have stood for it and would never have stayed if things had not been run as well as they could currently manage.

Their men had good wages, pithead baths, and Jonas looked after the few miners who were ever injured or sick. Things would have been different throughout the industry if the owners had been better masters – and as good as Jonas.

Jonas had few friends in the industry because he was impatient with those who would not change. It was just as well, Sep thought, that they were all staying, to keep things the way they had managed them so far and to do such vital work. He knew he should be glad of it instead of thinking he might have chosen another option. In war you rarely got to choose anything, he was sure. You did the best you could at the thing you were best at and hoped things would work out.

At first Cuthbert thought he should have become an officer. He seemed to have more in common with those who were than with the ordinary soldiers, but after a few days he felt differently. He was no more like these men than he was like anybody else and he could not have told anybody to do anything as he had no experience. He had to admit to himself that he had no experience of how other men lived at all, he knew so little of them, so little of anybody and the idea of responsibility for anybody else's life horrified him.

All he had to do was thicken his northern accent and lose himself among the other men. He was just the same as they were because of the uniform. How many men like him were hiding in such disguise? He was not unhappy, that was the strange thing. He had hated leaving home, having nobody to leave from, nobody to tell other than the women who cleaned his house. He regretted the comfort, the solitariness which he had grown used to. He could not imagine what it would be like living with a lot of common men. The very idea made him shudder.

He went to France. He remembered having been there when he was a small boy with his parents, just before his father died. He had distant memories of men fishing in a wide river, the smell of bread in the mornings, fresh vegetables from the kitchen garden left by the door in a wide basket, sitting outside in the evenings. He must have learned some basic French in the past because the language, right from the beginning, came back to him.

The other men were rather proud of his ability and would get him to interpret whenever they needed anything. Nobody had ever looked admiringly at him before for any reason and he rather liked it. They also did not seem to mind that he was different, there were so many misfits in the army, everybody was different.

It was strange being in France but not on holiday. There was nothing to do to begin with and the weather was cool. He had thought he would regret leaving the dale but all he missed was Rose Grant and he had seen so little of her that it was not as hard as he had thought it would be. He had not known how lonely he was before now and hadn't dared to admit to himself how alone he felt. Not just since his mother died, always.

The other men accepted him as they accepted one another and since they were all local men in his Durham Light Infantry Battalion it was like being in a gang when you were a small boy. He had never been in a gang before and although he knew that war was a serious and dangerous thing he was – he could have laughed – a natural soldier, even his sergeant said so.

He was naturally immaculately neat in everything he did, obeyed orders instantly – shades of his mother there – and was praised for his shooting ability. He did not like to say that his father had taught him to shoot when he was a little boy, it was one of the few clear and good memories: the fells, the chase, the dogs, the cold still afternoons and bearing the single bird back in triumph for his mother to hang in the pantry for several days before it was cooked for supper.

The men asked him about his life, much of which he was obliged to invent. It was a lovely life, he thought, with a secret smile. He was married to Rose. He even had a photograph of her to show them. It was not a recent photograph, it must have been taken when she was first married, he thought, and was ashamed that he had stolen it, filched it from the desk when she was not looking.

It had been lying there on top of a pile he thought she had possibly been sorting through when she was moving and obliged to throw things out that she no longer considered essential. She had been making tea for him when he put it into his breast pocket. He was so glad that he had done it. Every night he looked at it, even kissed it. Other men showed him photographs of their wives and children. He just wished he had a photograph of Maddy when she was little; she could have been his small daughter. It would have been so nice, he thought.

They were based just outside Lille, close enough to go there when they had time off. Lille had bars, cinemas and theatres and was a pleasant place to go when he had free time and it was good to go there with the other men, he enjoyed being with them.

The main task he and the other men had was digging trenches and he had never done hard physical work before, he had never done any kind of work at all and it was rather a shock. For the first day or two it was invigorating, a kind of release somehow, it made him feel needed and worthwhile. After that the blisters on his hands broke and bled and the digging was hell. Each day a new trial.

He learned to curse and swear in broad Durham with a little humour like the others. It was difficult to be miserable with Nobby from Sunderland raving about his football team and Jack, who was from Sherburn Village, just outside Durham and had five kids and one on the way, saying he was glad to get out of it all.

Cuthbert's hands hardened, he got used to being called

'Bert' and even liked it and remembered who he was after the first few times of thinking somebody else was being spoken to. Whatever hell war was, and he found a lot of it difficult, they were all sharing it together which was a new experience for him and made things much easier.

Winter set in and then he remembered his big stone house, his huge log fires but he did not feel like that on Christmas Day. The last Christmas had been one of the loneliest days of his life. He had not seen anybody, had not ventured out during the day in case people should pity him and feel obliged to ask him to share their day. He had gone for a long walk at dusk and had avoided speaking to anybody. He had just waited for it to be over and what a relief it had been to wake on Boxing Day and know he was not to go through it again.

This Christmas Day the nurses who were stationed locally came over for the occasion.

'Don't you ask anybody to dance?' one bold pretty girl had complained.

'I can't dance.'

She insisted on teaching him to waltz and other nurses joined in with enthusiasm, treating him to the quick step. One or two seemed sorry to find that he was married. Cuthbert liked being popular. He did not 'fancy' any of them as the men called it, his only love was Rose, but he liked the attention, the laughter and the dancing.

He knew nothing of war, he trusted the officers and the commanders, and it was easy for him to let someone else shoulder the burden while he did what he was told. He could not believe that he had done nothing with his life before this, that he had had no ambitions.

It was a strange kind of war with nothing to do. Some of the younger men talked of it being over soon. The older ones said little. Cuthbert learned to take things day by day. He wanted to write to Rose, but he had no excuse and he was afraid that someone would find out that they were not married. At night, when he could not sleep, he composed the letters he would have liked to send to her and he even answered them sometimes.

She told him how much she missed him, that she loved him, how Maddy was hard at work at Black's Foundry in Durham where they turned out castings for the navy and what they were doing towards the war effort and just before he went to sleep he pictured his homecoming.

It would be full summer in the dale, long blue and white days, short warm nights, gentle rain falling on the windows lulling Rose to sleep as he returned to her. She would meet him where the road left the village to wind down the rest of the dale and up into the Durham coalfield.

He pictured her standing there, arms folded, smile ready with the little stone houses behind her and the hills reaching up on either side, the grass green as surely it never was anywhere else, the sheep like cream spots here and there and the higgledy-piggledy stone walls dividing up like a quilt on a bed. She was waiting for him, always when he went to sleep he could picture her intent and slightly worried face and how as she saw him her expression changed, turned to delight, her eyes shining, her mouth smiling, her arms held out towards him.

The British Expeditionary Force sat in the trenches they had dug and heard how Hitler was making his way through Belgium and Holland and now was coming into France. It felt like the whole world was on the move. As they sat there in the darkness the sound of many feet came past and they realized at daybreak that the French army were in retreat.

The roads were soon filled with civilians trying to get out of the way of the encroaching German army, the German aircraft shooting at anything at all it seemed to Bert. It was indiscriminate. Even worse than that, he thought.

The word came that they were to retreat.

'And not a minute too soon,' Jack said, throwing down the remains of his Woodbine. 'Let's get the hell out of here.'

There was total disarray. The road became blocked with lorries which had been abandoned and in any case the roads were not safe with the Germans dive-bombing from above.

They were told to make for Dunkirk but how to get there

they were not sure. They managed as best they could across the fields and then the canal. They clung to what remained of the bridge there which was badly damaged and made their way across and soon they were almost into Dunkirk Harbour.

He never forgot the sight of it, the men waiting there, the ships and small boats coming to the rescue. German aeroplanes had already sunk one large ship and a lot of men were standing in the water, some just with their heads showing, so eager were they to get away.

Destroyers were waiting further out and the little boats were coming into the beaches where thousands of men were waiting and hoping, coming in again and again and picking up as many men as they could manage without sinking. There were dead and injured men on the beach.

Jack, Nobby and Bert made their way into the water and just as they were about to be picked up a German aeroplane dive-bombed and Nobby cried out as he was hit, and Jack and Bert helped him into the boat. It was only then that Bert realized Jack had been hit too.

'I'm all right,' Jack assured him.

Nobby was not all right. He was dead by the time they got to the destroyer.

The Germans followed them all the way home to the white cliffs of Dover. Bert had never been so glad to see them and he was so sorry that his friend had died so close to being rescued. It made him want to cry though he had not cried in years.

Once in England they were given cups of tea and sandwiches, and then he managed to find the right train to take him to King's Cross. It was a long and lonely journey home. There was nobody to meet him, nobody to care. The trains were full everywhere and he was obliged to sit on the floor. He could no longer think about Nobby. He was so tired that he went to sleep and the comforting sound of the train rocked him gently.

Fifteen

It was a beautiful summer's day in the dale. Rose heard a banging on the door and opened it to a man she didn't recognize and if she had been like a lot of women she would have screamed. He was dishevelled to the point of being unkempt. Was he a tramp? Beneath the general appearance she discerned a uniform of some kind and somewhere she could see eyes she knew but only just because they were almost lost in the tiredness of his face.

'Rose?' he said faintly.

She stared.

'Why, Mr Felix.' He had never called her Rose before. 'We were wondering about you. We've been hearing the most awful stories about what happened in France and I knew you must be caught up in it. I was worried that you might not make it back, that you might have been killed.'

'I know I . . . I shouldn't have come here but I . . .' He almost smiled. 'I don't seem to be able to get into my house. I haven't slept much and I haven't eaten much and . . .'

'Come in, come in.'

Somehow he managed, stumbling, and after that she set up the tin bath in the kitchen surrounded by a clothes horse draped with sheets for privacy. She watched him take off his boots, and they fell apart as he did so. His feet were bloody. She started towards him and he put up one hand.

'I'll be all right,' he said.

'You will be nothing of the sort,' Rose said.

She sat him down and bathed his feet, put ointment on them and made him comfortable.

She gave him tea and bread and jam and promised him

stew as soon as it could be ready. He nodded without saying anything.

As he gratefully discarded his clothes she took them and made the best of them she could while hunting out the few things of Bradley's that she had retained from nothing but sentiment.

When he was washed, dry and changed, and she had cleared everything away, she noticed that the clothes hung on him as he'd lost so much weight. Later she fed him stew and then, despite his tired protests, she found him some of Bradley's old pyjamas in the back of a wardrobe – where on earth had they come from? she wondered. She thought she had got rid of everything like that – and put him into her bed and closed the curtains and left him there.

She slept in the other room with Maddy but was a little worried about telling her that Mr Felix was staying there. She blurted it all out when Maddy returned home.

'He couldn't have gone home, could he?' Maddy said. 'He hasn't got anybody there. He did right to come to us. What an awful experience for them.'

Rose was so grateful to her understanding daughter but she couldn't sleep thinking of how he had come to her rather than to anybody else, remembering the state of his feet and how exhausted he had been. He emerged the following day just before lunchtime. She was bustling about in the kitchen. Now clean and refreshed she could still see how gaunt he was, the hollows under his eyes and his wrists which were so bony.

She gave him breakfast and only when he had eaten and had two big cups of tea did she venture to ask, 'Was it very bad?'

'Yes, it was dreadful, not for me, of course. I'm here, I'm lucky but for others . . .' and he told her a little about it but not too much. She sensed he did not want to distress her. 'Thousands of refuges on the road, nowhere to go and they couldn't stay because of the Germans. They had us cornered, you see, backed us right up to the coast and on to the beaches.' He stopped there. 'You haven't changed. I thought about you and Maddy such a lot.'

'Oh, well, Maddy is working all hours at Black's Foundry and we are doing what we can.'

'I'm sure you are. I should go. Thank you so much, Rose. I'm so grateful to you for everything you've done for me. May I call you Rose?'

'Why, yes, of course.'

'You can hardly call me Cuthbert though,' he said with a glimpse of humour. 'It is a shockingly dreadful name. I suppose Bert would do if you could bring yourself to say it.'

'Mr Felix—'

'Oh, please, I've been Bert in the army and I'm used to it. I tried not to tell them my real name. I blame my mother.'

'People always blame their mothers.'

'We have to blame somebody, I suppose. Thank you so much. I don't know what I would have done otherwise.'

'This is your home. Everybody here knows you. They would all have taken you in.'

He couldn't tell her that he wouldn't have gone to anybody else in the village, that he felt nothing for any of them and that it really felt like home now that she had helped and looked after him.

Bert staggered home. It was not tiredness any more, it was just that he felt so much for Rose Grant and he could not find any words for what he wanted to say to her. All through the hell of France he had sworn to himself that if he got through he would go to her and ask her to be his wife, but now he hadn't had the courage to do it.

There he found the key he could not find the day before, where it had always been, where it should be, under the stone beside the door. He was certain it had not been there the day before, but maybe in his distress he had not been able to see it or perhaps subconsciously he had longed to go to her and could not help himself.

He stepped inside his house and stared. How could he have lived in such a place as this? It was a monstrosity filled with his mother's possessions. There was nothing that he had chosen, nothing that he had liked.

It was dusty and the hall was dark and gloomy. There were awful pictures on the walls of cottages and unlikely shepherdesses and ugly huge vases on small delicate tables.

He went from room to room like a critical visitor, amazed. It was huge and could easily have housed a family of ten; there were six bedrooms, three reception rooms. The curtains were drawn and he quickly pulled them aside to let in the summer sunshine. There were Holland covers over everything and these he cast aside only wishing he hadn't because the furniture underneath was years and years old and it reminded him of his mother and of the life they had led together.

It was rich, glittering even in the morning sun, and it made him want to sit down and cry. But he didn't have the energy to do that. Instead he went and lay down on the bed with the sunshine pouring through the window. The bed felt like a cloud and he was very soon fast asleep.

Phoebe Robson followed Rose into the front room of the little cottage.

'I understand Cuthbert Felix is back. Will saw him. Is he here?'

'No, he went home.'

'Ah, yes, I think he was just going in his front door earlier, but you've seen him of course.'

'Yes, I have. He told me how awful France had been and the soldiers in retreat.'

'It's very worrying,' Phoebe said. 'Whatever will happen now? Hitler will be here in no time and then what will we do?'

Rose had no idea, but just then she couldn't think of anyone but Bert. Would she ever get used to calling him that?

'I didn't know you were such good friends with Mr Felix,' Phoebe said.

'I think I was just the first person he thought of when he got here, the house is the first you come to and . . . would you like tea, Phoebe?'

'Thank you. He stayed here.'

It was not quite a question and Rose wanted to say vulgar rude things because Phoebe had no right to make insinuations of any kind, especially about a man who was years younger than she was, a man who had suffered much, who needed some kindness from anyone who would aid him. She did not tell Phoebe that she had not changed the sheets and that she could smell his scent mixed with her good soap on the pillows and that it made her think of Bradley somehow and cry a little.

'He was finished,' she said. 'Worn out.'

'I could never understand what he was doing, joining up like that. He could have been an officer. He's an educated well-thought-of man. It's the duty of men like that to take on the responsibility of war.'

Rose thought she could hear Will Robson talking to his wife in Phoebe's speech.

'People know what they can manage. We aren't all born for the same thing,' she said.

'The village will talk you know, about you taking him in.'

'Not if you and Will don't say anything.'

'I doubt he was the only one to see you letting him into your house.'

Rose could not help thinking that she had never really liked Phoebe very much, but there was just sufficient truth in Phoebe's insinuations for her to blush and turn away. She must not think of him; the way the sunlight turned his hair golden, the beginning of hope dawning again in his eyes when he had gone off back to his own house this morning, how pleased and grateful he was at everything she did for him.

He would be staying only a few days, she knew, and then he would have to go back to war. She could not think how awful that must be, especially as he had no one to leave behind, nobody to care about, no one to do his packing and ask whether he had with him all that he needed. She found herself wishing she could be there or he could be here and she realized that she had been on her own for far too long, dreaming stupid dreams about a man she cared nothing for, who cared nothing for her.

Rose thought he would be hurt that she might think of him in such a way and banished him from her mind, but when he left she wished him well. It was an awful thing to have to admit but she was relieved when he had gone because she could not stop thinking about him, wanting to run to him, to make more of their friendship than there was. She was ashamed of herself for thinking about what his body might feel like under her fingers.

After a week, when he could get his shoes back on with the minimum of discomfort Bert made his way over to Edgar Ward's office and made an appointment to see him.

He thought Edgar looked old but of course he must be getting on towards retiring age. Edgar, like him, had nothing to retire to. His wife and son were long since gone. How lonely he must be. Except that I'm not now, Bert thought. I'm not lonely any more.

'I want to make a will,' he said, seating himself in Edgar's gloomy office. He had been in there a great many times but had never thought until today how beautiful the view was from the window. He got up to look. It was full summer in the dale and the grass rippled in the slight breeze.

It was stuffy in Edgar's office. Edgar looked pleased. After Bert's mother had died Edgar had urged him to make a will but he had said he had no one to leave his money to and did not care what happened.

'Have you ever thought of opening this window?' Bert said, before he could stop himself.

Edgar stared at him.

'Mr Felix—'

'Why don't you call me Bert? You've known me since I was a little boy.'

Bert sat back down again.

'I understand that things were very difficult,' Edgar said. 'The retreat . . .'

Bert thought of Nobby dying in Dunkirk harbour, of the dead soldiers on the beach, of the old people, the children shot by German planes on the roads, the bombs leaving huge craters on the beaches. He thought of the destroyers trying to distract the German aeroplanes from the little boats, of the way some men had tried to carry booze and cigarettes on to the little boats and how everything was taken off them because of the weight. Did they not think another man might be saved if they didn't do such daft things?

He thought of how the infantry shot down an aeroplane with rifles and how the men had cheered. He thought of the officer on the ship which brought them home, who had tried to take the bunk of a badly hurt boy and how the other soldiers had stopped him. So many memories, so many friends dead in France and yet in some stupid way he longed for his friends, would be glad to go back.

'I want to leave everything to Rose Grant,' Bert said.

It made him want to laugh, Edgar's expression. He didn't speak at first. He just looked amazed and then embarrassed before his solicitor's face took over and blanked everything out and even then he said, 'Rose Grant?' as though it was the most ridiculous thing he had ever heard.

Bert wanted to blush and he would have done before his spell in the army but nothing would have made him do so now. He looked calmly back across the desk at Edgar and held his stare until Edgar went silent.

'I don't want anybody to know about this,' Bert said.

Edgar was once more the professional.

'It goes without saying,' he said.

'Sometimes things need to be said,' Bert said. 'I want her to be comfortable and not to have to worry about anything. She's had a bad time over a number of years. Nobody helped her. Gilbert Taylor and Will Robson were good friends of her husband but when she lost her house nobody lifted a finger. I can't say they've been much good to her since.'

'I'm sure they did what they could.'

'No, they didn't. None of you did,' Bert said roundly. 'He would have been ashamed of you all for the way that this village treated his family after he was dead when his family had lived here for so long. I'm ashamed for me but more ashamed for the rest of you. I'll be leaving in a few days so I want that doing as soon as you can. I'll come back and sign it once it's sorted out.'

He got up and walked out, leaving Edgar staring after him. He could not help enjoying his moment of triumphing in a small way over Edgar and, it seemed to him, over the village too.

He had never been afraid of dying before. Now he was. He didn't want to leave Rose. If he came back he would ask her to marry him. No, he thought, when I come back. I have a purpose now, my life has meaning. I love a wonderful woman. He didn't like to think there was a possibility that she did not love him so he did not give the matter any more thought, he just remembered the photograph which he always carried in his breast pocket. He called himself silly and sentimental but it meant a great deal to him now.

Bert left the village without meeting anyone, without seeing anyone. The gardens of his house were completely overgrown, there was nobody to tend to them; the two women who looked after his house were away. He presumed they had probably gone to work in the munitions factory in Aycliffe. He left the house only to buy food when Mr Wilson's shop was quiet and there was nobody in it. He barely spoke and Mr Wilson didn't say anything.

He paid for what he bought and then he went home and ate it and when the time came he left the village, thinking about Rose and wishing he could have been braver and gone to her and asked . . . for what? He didn't know.

He couldn't ask her to marry him as he worried she would laugh. He couldn't ask her to sleep with him, it wasn't decent and it would destroy her reputation in such a small place. He couldn't even risk being seen there more than once or twice. How could he say anything? He was the worst of men when it came to speech, but he treasured, and held to him through the days, thoughts of her kindness, her smile, the way that she had looked after him.

She was his first thought when he awoke and his last when he slept. It made him smile just to think of her beautiful gentle face and after that he thought it would not be long until this was all over. When the war is over, he kept saying to himself, if I get back, when this is all finished, then I'll ask her.

He went away. Rose didn't know where he had gone. She would have given a great deal to have known but there was no one to ask, and she did not like to give people the idea that she was thinking about him. They would label her middle aged, no, worse, 'a woman of a certain age'. It was a horrid expression.

He was her own private world. She was obliged to invent most of it and apologize to him in her mind as she thought about him. It was doing no harm and in any case, he had no one else to think about him. She thought he might find some young woman he loved and although she was envious and hated this in one way she wanted him to be happy and maybe to get married and have children. Everybody should have that, after all.

She told herself she would be pleased when he did find someone he loved. She had had Bradley. As far as she knew Cuthbert had had no one and everyone was entitled to a true love. She wished him well wherever he was and hoped that he would come back. So many young men had been killed.

Rose was not at all prepared for the letter which came to her. All it said was that Bert was a prisoner of war of the Japanese and that he was well.

Rose had to sit down while she read it over and over again. He had been allowed to send it and he was safe. Or was he? She could not even cry. Maddy was in the kitchen and she would feel foolish and have to explain herself. Why had she been sent this? And then she knew why it was. He had no one else to send the message to.

She was so glad that he had thought of her, that he had reached out to her in this way. Should she tell other people? Would they wonder what was going on? Did anybody care? She didn't think they did. She said nothing but kept the letter under her pillow and each night she prayed for Bert and each night when she had gone to bed she thought of him and sometimes she cried.

The war, she thought, was going to go on for ever. She started to think she would die and the war would still be happening and she did not think that she would ever see him again. Other men had leave, they parted, they came back and were jolly in spite of everything when their families saw them. Others, of course, did not. Some families had lost brothers, husbands, sons. She could say nothing. They thought she had nobody to lose.

She was beginning to feel as though she had lost Bert while never knowing him and the awful thing about it was that he might think of her as a replacement mother. His mother had not been like Rose, but she was generous enough to think that if he had done then she was glad that he had thought of her when he was captured. She hoped that he might think of her kindly now because she had taken him in, that however he imagined her she would be that person.

If he came back, if only he came back, she would greet him at a distance if he wanted it, she would be pleased and hold the hand of any woman he had chosen. She would support him in any way she could and just be so relieved if he just came back.

She could not bear that he should die and yet why should he not? Why should he be spared, why should she have the joy of a homecoming? She had not earned it. She had already had a husband and a child and she should be pleased because it was so much.

If he died she would live on for him and for Bradley. There was nothing else to do. It was the right thing. She would not feel sorry for the woman who had lost so much. So many people had lost in this war. Nobody was left untouched by it. Nobody would celebrate without a grief of some kind when it was over, if it ever was.

Time stretched itself out as it does when you are waiting. Rose was beginning to feel as though half her life had been spent in waiting. Maddy went to work and they cleaned the house, baked bread and tried to economize through the war. They did the things that women did when they could not go to war. They ate sparingly and grew vegetables in their tiny garden. Rose helped the various local farmers in the fields and she and the other women in the village raised money for aeroplanes and generally towards the war effort. She was very proud of her daughter for doing such an important job but everything they did was important and helped.

You could see the German aeroplanes in the sky from the countryside around Maddy's house when she stood outside on dark nights. They were looking for Consett Ironworks, she felt sure. So far they had not found it. It was well hidden in a dip in the land though she did not imagine when it had been first started in the mid-1800s they would have deliberately thought to hide it for fear of enemy attack by air.

David also said they used Durham Cathedral as a landmark, to turn off out and then head towards the coast to attempt to bomb the Sunderland shipyards where new ships for the navy were being built. Durham had not been bombed, she was thankful for that. And the fact that she could go to work each day and be useful to the war effort. She was glad, though she knew it was selfish, that David had not gone and she didn't think Sep would have either though she heard nothing from him. People who managed coal mines weren't going anywhere and people who ran shipyards and steel foundries weren't either, they were much too important at home. Nowhere was safe, she reminded herself, nobody would come out of this unscathed.

Halfway through the afternoon sirens screamed. Sep cursed. It had been a beautiful summer's day until then and things had been going well. You should never, he reminded himself, take these things for granted even for a second.

The first noise he heard after the sirens was the sound of the birds kicking up a tremendous fuss, followed by the sound of aircraft and then bombing. He couldn't believe it. Nothing like this had ever happened so close. Instead of taking shelter he went outside. The air was full of aeroplanes and the enemy aircraft were dropping bombs on the little town which was now his home. Why ever would they do such a thing? Were they trying to target the pits? It could be their only reason for doing so but it was such a small target. They were a long way from the Newcastle shipyards.

Their accuracy was dismaying. The noise of the planes and the impact as the bombs hit the houses was deafening and the debris and dust flew up. It did not last long but it felt like an eternity and he was aware all the time that he could do nothing but watch as the miners' houses were reduced to rubble. Not for the first time Sep wished he could have joined the air force, done something tangible about it, get results, get rid of the enemy aircraft.

The spitfires from the local airfield were there now. The whole thing had turned into a dogfight but even as they retreated the enemy aircraft let the bombs fall on to the edge of the town and into the shallow water of the North Sea. The water parted, rose, the sound was huge but by then his ears had had more than they could stand. Two of the aircraft were shot down and rapidly sank. He could not tell which was which amid the dust and noise and sunlight and confusion.

To his dismay the edge of the town was bombed as well as the side near to the sea. He knew that Jonas had gone home for his dinner at midday and Mary was in the house and the dogs were there too. He began to run and did not stop until he came in sight of the house. Until then he had not realized how much Jonas and Mary meant to him. They were the family his father and mother had not been, and he could not bear to think that something might have happened to them.

The front door had been blown off, the glass had blown out of the windows and part of the building was completely destroyed. He stood in shock for what seemed like a long time but was probably no more than a few seconds and then ran in among the rubble.

As he did so the dogs hurtled towards him in the dust and he gained the dining room, stopping short when he saw two unconscious bodies, the room open to the sky, the wood from the rafters which were left already creaking. Mary was nearer. He picked her up and ran outside with her, not stopping to ascertain whether she was alive, afraid that the roof would collapse with Jonas still inside.

He could hear the sound of the rafters breaking and various bits of the ceiling crashing down. The dust made him cough and choke. He ran back and half carried, half dragged his uncle out from among the debris and the ruined furniture and the plaster because he was too big to lift.

He heard the rest of the roof give way and fall in as he pulled Jonas clear through the front door. The smell from the rubble and the dust covered the whole area. He caught his breath and then went back to Mary's inert body.

'Mary?' Sep looked anxiously into her white face. She opened her eyes. 'Where are you hurt?'

She sat up and noticed she was bleeding from one arm. She blinked, coughed, tried to speak and after a moment or two all she said was, 'Jonas?'

Sep looked anxiously across. Jonas was not moving.

'Are you all right?'

All she could do was nod for a second or two and then she asked hoarsely, 'Is he dead?'

Sep went over and there his uncle lay quite still with his eyes closed. He didn't like to move him. He was just debating whether to run for help when his uncle stirred.

'No, I'm not dead,' came his surprisingly clear voice. 'I just wish they'd waited until I ate my dinner.'

Sep laughed in relief.

'The house is wrecked,' he said and the dogs both came over and licked Jonas's face until he protested but there was joy in his voice.

A dozen people died that day in the little pit town, every family was affected. Jonas's response was to raise and provide money to buy another Spitfire. God knows, Sep thought, we need them.

Rain. Not the kind of rain you got in England. Bert thought back to what pleasant memories he could think of to how English people talked about the rain. First it was just a large puddle beside the huts and then it was, as people thought of the day of judgement, continuous, it went on and on as if it would never stop. The huts flooded, the water got deeper and deeper and there were so many men in the huts that there was scarcely any room to move. The storm blew the roof off his particular hut and by then nobody cared. He began to feel as though he had always felt like this, as though there had never been anything but a world that was full of water.

They worked in the rain, making the road which the Japanese officers had decided was important. They worked virtually naked since they had no clothes any more; it was miserable and the guards screamed at them.

Bert did not see how any of them would survive. Around him his friends were sick, so ill that they could not stand. Some of them had one disease, some of them had many, great sores on their legs, typhus, malaria and were suffering from ordinary things like exhaustion and malnutrition. They had so little to eat, nothing but rice.

He did not recognize so many of the men who worked with him on the road. He tried not to think beyond the day. He thought about Rose. Each and every day he thought about what it would be like in Weardale and about how he must live so that he could get back to Rose. He thought of Maddy on her way to the office at Black's Foundry where he guessed they would be working flat out to keep the navy going. He thought of Maddy making food for herself and her mother.

He rarely spoke any more. He could barely remember the sound of his own voice. He dreamed of Rose's kitchen. He had not had a proper meal in almost four years. The work went on and on. He began to think he would die there as so many of his friends had died but he refused to let himself.

He thought he must have been insane to make his will. It had seemed like a good idea at the time and if he had been killed, drowned in a ship that went down, or shot by the enemy cleanly then yes, he could imagine dying in such a way but to die of work and near starvation – he could not let it happen. He would do everything he could to stay alive.

Rose held the letter in her hands. The war was over and she had waited and waited for news, for Bert to still be alive, for something good to happen. Other people rejoiced. She waited and began to despair. She thought her life was over. What would she do if he did not come back?

She had given up hope. It was September and the war was over when the letter came. He was alive. He was alive and coming back to her. She did not know when it would be, he had to come back to England and he had been in hospital abroad and might have to stay in hospital when he came home. She prayed that he would come back after his dreadful experiences.

Then one day, when for once she was not expecting it and not thinking about him, there was a knocking on her front door and when she opened it a skeletal man stood there. She stared at his sunken cheeks and eyes and it was several seconds before she recognized him.

'Bert?'

'Yes, it's me.'

She stared even more.

'I'm all right,' he said. 'Really, Rose, I'm going to be all right.'

She started to cry and that was when he got hold of her for the first time and he said, 'You can't think how much I wanted to come back to you,' and then he let go of her and said apologetically, 'You don't mind me saying that?'

'I don't mind at all. Do come in.'

She sat him down by the fire, and then she fed him. It would take a lot of meals before he would put on a decent amount of weight.

'I'm so very glad to see you.'

'Are you?' He looked anxiously at her.

'Yes, of course. Everybody will be.'

He sat for a few moments and then he looked straight at her and he said, 'I've thought about nothing but you. I love you, Rose. I've always loved you.'

Rose blushed. She didn't know what to say.

'When I was away, all that time, I thought if I was as lucky as to come back – and I know how many people haven't – that I would ask you to marry me.' He put up a hand as Rose stuttered. 'I don't want an answer now. I want you to think about it. I won't take it amiss if you turn me down – at least I will but I don't want you to think about that aspect, I just want you to consider if you might be able to. Now I'm going to my house because I want you to think very carefully about it. I don't want to get in the way. Let me know when you've thought.' He then calmly got to his feet.

'I'll let you know tonight. Come back at about seven.'

'I will,' he said and walked out.

'He asked you to marry him?'

Maddy stared. She had come home from work to find her mother in what was described best as 'a proper tizz', all pink cheeked and shiny eyed and confused and unable to sit still for a second.

'Yes. He's just come back and he came straight to me and . . . I don't know what to think or what to say.'

Her mother looked . . . what did she look like? Maddy wondered. Was she embarrassed or excited? She looked almost like a young girl, shy about the idea but half hoping somebody was going to say to her that they were glad for her, happy, wanted her to get married. Maddy was jealous. How awful, she thought, going hot with shame.

Rose didn't say anything, as though she was not entitled to anybody wanting to marry her, as though she had never expected such a thing.

'And do you want to marry him?' It seemed suddenly such an intimate thing to say especially when the blush formed on her mother's neck and progressed so much that Rose turned from her and pretended to be doing something.

'I can't believe he asked me,' Rose said. 'People will talk. He's a lot younger than me.'

'Does that matter?'

'I like him,' her mother said and the three words held an almost musical quality. 'Do you know what it is, Maddy, it's the way that his hair falls across his brow. Isn't that ridiculous? He has straight golden hair and it is so very attractive when it shades his eyes. He has beautiful eyes.'

Her mother, Maddy thought in wonder, was in love and why should she not be? Why should her mother not marry the strange man who had no friends? He had plenty of money, had a fine house and he must be in love with her mother. He could have had no other motive in asking her to marry him.

'Have you said yes?'

Her mother looked at her.

'Not yet.'

'Why not? You care about him, he cares about you.'

'I was thinking about you.'

'There's no need to consider me. I have been thinking that I might rent a nice little house in Durham.'

'But Maddy . . . You can't go and live on your own in Durham, I would hate to think of you stuck somewhere by yourself, I would never let you do it. You will come and live with Bert and me. I think you would have been married to Sep Ward if I had left you alone long before now and you aren't . . .' Her mother stopped short of calling her an old maid Maddy was glad to hear.

'No, you were right,' Maddy said bravely. 'It would never have worked out.'

'But you haven't met anybody else?' Her mother looked hopefully at her but Maddy could not say that she had, she wished she could have.

'And I don't want to upset you.'

Maddy hugged her.

'You haven't,' she said. 'If you want to marry him please go ahead and do so. He's a nice man and I like him and I'll be happy to dance at your wedding.'

'Are you sure?'

'Quite sure.'

Maddy pushed from her the jealous way she felt. She was glad that her mother was in love, that she was marrying the man she wanted, but part of Maddy wished she didn't have to share her mother with him. They had grown so close since her father had died. Everything would alter now and she was afraid of things changing. Every time things had changed they had got worse, but she must be hopeful for the future and her mother was entitled to some happiness. She would get used to the idea in time but nothing would ever be the same again.

Bert sat over his fire imagining both Rose's acceptance and the consequences and her refusal and what would happen after that. He could not dare to think of the one or bear to think of the other. If she refused his life would be lonely and pointless. If she accepted he might never sit over the fire alone again. Would she want to bring Maddy to live with them?

Of course she would and he would be pleased to have them both there. He would like having the life, the noise, the laughter, the conversation, even the problems and he could lavish them with all the things they had never had like beautiful clothes and a car. Maddy wouldn't have to work any more, and he could take them to Newcastle to the theatre and to London and even to other places, exciting new places where none of them had ever been. Now he'd seen something of the world and had experienced life if she decided she didn't want to marry him then he would go off and make some kind of a life of his own. He knew that he could do anything now.

It was a long time before evening, when she had told him she would give him his answer, and as the time grew nearer so the wait became longer. In the end he was late by ten minutes because he was so worried and kept thinking he'd left the door open and the guard down from the fire and then he couldn't find his coat.

He ran the short distance from his house to hers and banged on the front door and Maddy let him in. Her face betrayed nothing. He found himself not knowing what to say, he managed to stutter good evening and she managed to tell him how glad she was that he had come home and that was as much as either of them achieved. She guided him into the front room and then disappeared.

He hovered in the doorway until Rose said, 'Do come in, Bert. Close the door, you're letting in the draught,' and he felt like a schoolboy, fell over his feet trying to shut the door, caught his coat in it, had to open the damned door to retrieve it and was red-faced, speechless with worry and fear, and couldn't look at her by the time the door was closed and he had turned to face her.

She didn't say anything and he couldn't tell anything by her demeanour.

'Do you know how old I am?' she said finally.

His heart sank, she was going to turn him down for a ridiculous reason like age.

'I don't care how old you are,' he said flatly.

'Or that people may talk?'

He thought back to Thailand, to the camps, to the work and the heat and the hunger and the men who had died and the Japs' inhuman treatment.

'I've long since stopped worrying about things like that. I don't care,' he said. 'I love you, Rose. I've always loved you. Marry me, please. Put me out of my misery.'

She laughed. He liked it when she laughed. He had remembered during the awful times what it was like when she laughed and sometimes it had been the only thing he had to hold on to. It was the sweetest sound he thought he had ever heard.

'Don't you love me, Rose?' he pleaded, unable to bear the thought that she might escape him now after all they had been through.

'Oh, yes,' she said and somehow after that, in those few seconds that followed, he was happier than he had ever been in his life.

He went over and kissed her. Her lips were dry like flowers that hadn't had any water and her breath was sweet and uneven and her hair felt like kid gloves in his fingers. He drew her to him and her body was soft and fitted against his as he had always known it would and she yielded in his arms as he was sure she had not done since Bradley Grant had died. He had always envied Bradley, now he was sorry for him and for all the people who were not loved by

Rose. He was the luckiest man in the world, he had come home.

Rose couldn't sleep. And at first she couldn't admit to herself that she couldn't sleep because she wanted Bert. She wanted him as much as she had wanted Bradley in the past and that felt like a betrayal and then the feeling passed like the lust had overwhelmed it and she had the sense to be glad.

She wished to dance around the room, to run over to his house and throw herself at him and when she could not rid herself of the idea she waited until first light and then she dressed and ran along the street. Luckily it was early, there was nobody about and she banged on his door. There was a long silence and she almost ran away, but she made herself stay, thinking it was a big house and it would take him time to get to the door no matter how hard someone knocked upon it.

He looked surprised when he opened it and he was not even dressed. Rose didn't give him time to say anything. She kissed him, she moved him back into the hall and kissed him again and then she said, 'I want to go to bed with you, Bert. Right now.'

He laughed with joy.

'It is all right, isn't it?' she asked.

'Rose, I've wanted to go to bed with you for the last ten years at least,' and then she laughed and they put an arm around each other and walked upstairs together.

Since she had first moved into the village as a widow her friend had rarely visited Rose. Now, only five days after Bert had come back, Phoebe came to the little cottage looking eagerly about her and accepted Rose's offer of tea.

As they sat down Phoebe said, 'I heard a rumour in the village that I'm sure can't be true.'

'Really?' Rose fussed with tea and cakes and didn't look in her visitor's direction especially since she was sure that people would somehow realize she and Bert were sharing a bed.

'Yes.' Not getting any help, Phoebe plunged in. 'That

you are considering marrying Cuthbert Felix. I know it can't be true, that he would never ask somebody who is old enough to be his mother and that you would never consider the insult to Bradley's memory by marrying again but I heard such tales.' She laughed.

Rose thought happily of Phoebe's husband, middle aged and getting tubby and of Bert, slender, younger, and she put forward her left hand where as well as Bradley's wedding band there gleamed the big square ruby which Bert had bought for her when he had taken her into Newcastle.

'Yes, I'm going to marry him. Hasn't he bought me the most beautiful ring on earth? You and Will are invited to the wedding of course.'

'It's true then?' Her guest was open mouthed.

'Oh, yes,' Rose said and although she knew it was shameful she could not help thinking of Bert's house, the biggest and most elegant house in the district, and be glad.

Sixteen

All those times when Maddy could have gone to parties which the Blacks had and had never invited her to and it had come to this.

David saying to her, 'I'm getting married to Ella Welsh. We'd very much like you to come to the wedding.'

Maddy's face was stiff with grief. All the daydreams of David walking her back down the aisle while his family and hers looked on, smiling, crumbled under his happy gaze. Even then she acknowledged to herself that it was as much for what he was as who he was. David was respectable, his father was admired and loved by the people of the city because he had helped them so many times.

She so much wanted to be a part of his family and now she never would. She knew that he had been seeing Ella Welsh for some time, but David was attractive and he'd had several girlfriends that she knew of. She had never given up hope. Now she did and afterwards, when she went home, she endured the evening and only in bed did she allow the tears to spill.

It was typical of Iris to come to her at the wedding and say, 'I didn't realize you'd been invited.'

'Hello, Iris,' Maddy said, looking beyond her in a way that she hoped was rude.

Mrs Black ignored her other than a polite smile and Mr Black was too busy to talk to her. Maddy felt so left out, so unwanted, she didn't know anybody there, people didn't seem to realize that she was alone.

Standing outside the church however a voice behind her said her name and when she turned around Sep was standing there. Behind him, not far off, stood an older man whom she guessed to be his uncle Jonas. The likeness was so obvious that Sep could have been Jonas's son. Dressed in a dark suit Sep looked nothing like his father now. He was tall and elegant. Maddy stared, shocked. She had not thought he knew the Black family, it had never occurred to her that he might be there.

'Hello,' he said. 'How are you?'

Jonas Ward was not turned in her direction so thankfully she didn't have to speak to him.

'I'm very well, thank you,' she said, and moved away.

The reception was at the house and there was still rationing, but Mr Black said he had been saving several bottles of champagne for just such an occasion so people drank champagne and ate tiny sandwiches and the atmosphere was relaxed.

Maddy had not had champagne before and thought it quite strange stuff and rather disappointing. She talked to people though she did not remember what she said and she was aware all the time of the tall man in the dark suit who had once been hers. She was not sure she could believe it now.

'Shall I get you another glass of champagne?' Sep offered as he came up to her.

'No, thank you.'

He hesitated.

'I'm not sure what you think was my fault, but does it matter now?'

'Nothing was your fault,' she said.

Normally she wouldn't have said anything of the kind and blamed the champagne for her loose tongue.

'Was it David Black?'

'What?' She looked at him. Sep looked away.

'You fell in love with him.'

She couldn't tell him that she had fallen in love with Sep, long before she had known David Black when they were young and he was just there, around, and she had thought he always would be. It was the first time in years she had admitted to herself how important Sep was to her, how important he had always been.

'I suppose a little. He was an ideal.'

'A little?' Sep looked surprised and not very pleased. 'You turned me down because of him.'

'I did nothing of the kind. Whatever made you think that?'

'It's the truth. That and the fact that I wasn't going to be a solicitor. I hadn't realized you cared about such things.'

Maddy was so angry that she wanted to hit him.

'What a dreadful thing to say. I am neither so mercenary nor so concerned with social appearances,' she said and stormed out.

Worse still he followed her into the garden.

'An ideal? You wanted to marry an ideal?'

Maddy said nothing.

'I wasn't good enough for you.'

'You certainly weren't,' Maddy said.

He was silenced, she could see. She had said too much and it was not fair, she knew that it was not. He had asked her to go with him, he had told her he loved her, that he wanted to marry her. It was just that she could not bear he should come back like this and still be important to her. She would not have it.

'I didn't mean to say that. I'm sorry.'

'No, no. I understand completely,' he said and then he went inside.

Sep didn't think Jonas had noticed anything, he didn't think Jonas was ever very observant until they were alone in the office on the Monday for the first time and Jonas was looking at some papers.

'Who was the pretty young woman with the red hair?' Jonas suddenly asked.

Sep looked at him. Jonas hadn't even looked up. When he didn't answer Jonas prompted him.

'At the wedding on Saturday. You spent time with her both in the house and in the garden so you must know her quite well.'

'Madeline Grant.'

That was when Jonas looked at him.

'Grant? Is she a Durham girl?'

'No, she comes from Sweet Wells.'

'Bradley Grant's daughter?'

'That's right.'

Jonas said nothing for a long time, it seemed, and then he said shortly, 'He was a fool.'

'She isn't.'

'You like her?'

Sep picked up the papers that Jonas had been looking at for him.

'I used to. When you offered me a job here I asked her to marry me, but she wouldn't come with me. She thinks I'm not good enough for her. She could be right.'

'So, she was the girl. These things matter in small communities where people have so very little to talk about and end up talking about one another. I've always thought it rather ridiculous.'

'It's all some people have.'

'Certainly your father is used to it.'

'Did you never like him?'

'We never liked one another, each thought the other was the favourite. I blame my mother, just as everyone always does.'

'I certainly blame mine,' Sep said, more frank than he was sure he should be.

'She had tried living with your father,' Jonas pointed out dryly.

'Didn't you think about marrying again?'

'I have Mary.'

'You haven't married her.'

'Like you, I did ask her.'

There was a smile about Jonas's lips which wasn't usually there so Sep ventured, 'What did she say?'

Jonas actually grinned. 'She said I'd be doing the same things I do now but I wouldn't get paid.'

'She doesn't care about status?'

'I don't think she cares about anything,' Jonas said.

'Except you.'

'If there had been a child I expect she would have

complied,' Jonas said, and sounded a little sad but then spoiled it by saying, 'If we'd been married we would have had to go to a great many dreadful parties but as it is there's just us. People long since stopped asking me anywhere because I would never go and the thing I like best is staying at home over the fire, drinking brandy with Mary.'

Perhaps Mary was sad too, but if so she didn't show it, and she didn't have a great deal to do as she had other women in the house whom she directed to do the work. Jonas must pay her a great deal of money for what she did, because she always wore expensive clothes and she came and went from the house without anybody's leave and she had her own car. She spent a great deal of time with Jonas in the evenings, in the little sitting room together.

She had her own rooms on the first storey, a sitting room, a bedroom and a bathroom. Presumably she spent the night with Jonas when she chose, Sep thought, and she might not have his name but she had his protection, she ran his house and she had the benefit of his money.

Seventeen

Sep had thought he would never go back to Sweet Wells. The little town seemed to exist now only in his dreams so he was not ready for the day Jonas called him through into the office and closed the door behind him. It was so long after the wedding that he had put Maddy from his mind and no longer had to because he did not think about her any more.

'I've got something to tell you,' Jonas said.

'Oh God, what is it?'

'Your father died.'

'Oh, hell.' Sep sat down suddenly on the nearest chair.

Jonas didn't say anything for a few seconds and then he said, 'Don't go feeling guilty about it.'

'I don't.'

'I have an inclination that you will because that's what people always do. It was his duty – and your mother's – to look after you and they didn't.'

'Yes, but—'

'No buts. That's what being an adult is all about. You were the child. You'll have your turn later, no doubt, to try being a parent. This was their problem. You don't have to go back if you don't want to. My solicitor will sort it all out for you.'

'I should go.'

'Make sure it's for you and not for him and that it's for the right reasons,' Jonas said. 'People will talk whether or not you go and if you didn't go when he was alive, there's no reason you should go now he's dead unless you really want to.'

Sep looked at him.

'You've really thought this through.'

'I went through exactly the same thing when my father died.'

'And did you go back?'

'I never went back.'

'Do you regret it?'

'No.'

Sep said nothing. He didn't know what to do.

'When everything is sorted legally you can sell the house and the business premises and whatever else is caught up in it all, but you don't have to do anything that you don't want to.'

That, Sep thought, was what you called parenting.

'You're very kind to me,' he managed.

Jonas didn't look at him. 'Somebody had to be,' he said gruffly. And then after a long pause he added, 'As far as I'm concerned you're my son. There's you and there's Mary and after that I don't give a shit about anybody.'

Sep drove back to Sweet Wells. He travelled in the middle of the week in the middle of the morning in a small black car in the hope that nobody would notice him. The solicitor had sent a key to the house but it was not his own house which he noticed as much as old Grant House because it was a fine autumn day and he could see its windows glinting from the top of the hill. Nobody had boarded them up again.

He didn't linger in the house which he hadn't lived in for a long period since he was seven, when his mother had left. It had never felt like home. He was surprised at how small it was, a terraced house with an office on the end of it. It was shabby and uncared for and it looked as though his father had just stepped out. He had apparently dropped down dead in his office next door. As I should have expected him to, Sep thought. Mrs Herries was no longer there. He hadn't heard anything about her in years.

As he stood there he heard a noise behind him and there the old housekeeper was, looking just the same, but rather fatter and red-faced as daleswomen often were from the fresh air. She was smiling slightly.

'I thought it was you,' she said.

'How are you, Mrs Herries?' he asked, coming forward and shaking her hand.

'I'm very well. It must be hard for you coming back.'

'Yes. It feels strange.'

'It must,' she said. 'He was a very lonely man, your father, he wouldn't let people close. We shouldn't speak ill of the dead but he could have had a lot of friends if he'd been different. He was always so aware of his position in the dale, all those secrets he knew about people, it must have made him want to keep his distance.'

'I suppose so.' Sep didn't know what to say. 'Is there anything you'd like? I'm getting rid of everything and—'

'Oh, no, no,' she said, as though she imagined he thought she might be there for what she could get.

'Just a minute,' Sep said, and he went through into the dining room and picked up the clock from the sideboard. 'Would you like this?'

'Oh, it's very fine,' she said.

'Do have it.'

'Well, I've always admired it.'

'Even better,' he said with relief.

He wasn't going to climb the hill to the house, but somehow he found himself half the way there. He told himself that he and Maddy had never been there in fine weather, it had been in the winter just after her father died, but somehow it was the same except that the house had deteriorated so much that he longed to make things better. The place was deserted.

The doors had gone and the sheep had been in there and left droppings and some enterprising farmer had been using it as a shelter over the winter no doubt, there were strings off bales of hay and pieces of straw were scattered in the sitting room and the piano was still there. The keys didn't play very well and the wind and rain had ruined the wood.

Tramps had no doubt been in too because there were the remains of fires in the downstairs rooms and several empty bottles, some of them broken and a few cigarettes ends. He could not help going from room to room and thinking what a good family home it could be and wondering whether Maddy ever went there now. No, he thought, she wouldn't. The memories must be unendurable.

He decided that he must go back for his father's funeral, but he made no provision for one of those awful affairs afterwards where he should feed the village and speak to people he hadn't seen in years. He didn't want to satisfy their curiosity and since the people who would come were all local there was no need to cater for anyone from outside.

It rained that day and he left it to the last minute to arrive so that there should be no one to greet him outside the church. He followed his father's coffin to the front looking neither to the right nor to the left and stood alone in the first pew. The church was packed, his father had been so well known.

Afterwards they drove to the cemetery and everybody came too. He was beginning to feel warmer towards them though he carefully did not look to see whether Maddy and her mother were there. Once his father was buried he merely nodded and smiled at people, but he did not stop to talk to anyone and he was shaking when he was driven away.

Eighteen

When the pits were nationalized Jonas had managed to ensure that Sep was kept on as manager, but he had said he didn't want to go on himself.

'Don't you want to be a part of it any more?'

'I've done enough. I'm going to rest now and eventually I'm going to travel. Mary and I are going to see the world.'

'What makes you think we can manage without you?' Sep said in a voice he realized was too loud because he was panicked at the idea of having to manage without Jonas. He was afraid.

'You'll do very well.'

'And where am I supposed to live?' Sep knew this wasn't fair. Jonas could sell this house, he owed nothing to Sep, and they had done so much for him to begin with, but Jonas looked surprised at the question.

'Why, here of course,' he said. 'The house is for you. I hope you will use it wisely and the money I'm giving you.'

'What?'

'Well, you have a woman you want to marry, don't you?' Jonas said.

Sep said nothing.

'I have a feeling it might have been my fault,' Jonas said, moving about as though he would rather have been somewhere else.

'What do you mean?'

'All those years ago with the girl you wanted to marry. I didn't realize who she was when you first said you wanted to marry her.'

'How on earth could it possibly have been your fault?'

Jonas managed to look shamefaced. Possibly, Sep thought, for the first time in his life.

'I own Grant House.'

Sep had a sudden bout of sympathy for the house.

It was so beautiful and it was definitely a place – and not a farm. It had never been a farm, always something more, always something better, a gentleman's residence was what it was.

'You own it?'

Jonas didn't look at him.

'I put Rose and her daughter out when Bradley died.'

'Why on earth did you do that?'

'Because I blamed her parents. I know it seems awful now, but I was so bitter. My wife was Rose's sister, Catherine. Rose was having a baby. They were both pregnant and Catherine didn't come back to Durham. Rose had begged her to stay there, I know she had, and Catherine didn't care for the city. She was more worried about Rose than coming back to me so she stayed on. If Rose had urged her to go back to me, her husband, things might have been different. The second baby – our baby – arrived early. There was a snowstorm and they couldn't summon help to the farm when my wife went into premature labour.

'She and the baby both died. I thought if she had been at home in Durham it would not have happened. I was young and very angry. Later Bradley became ill and couldn't work. He offered to sell me the house. I'd made a lot of money by then so I used the money I had made in the pits. I was good at it.

'Bradley had no money to keep that wretched house going. It had eaten up everything his family had made. So I bought it from him.'

'Maddy knew you owned it?'

'Yes, I suppose she would.'

'Why didn't she say so?'

'You're my nephew and now . . . You and I get on whereas you never got on with your father.'

'Almost as if I owned the house,' Sep said.

'You will,' Jonas said.

Sep looked at him.

'Everything I have is for you,' Jonas said.

'Don't say that.' Sep got up. 'You're not very old yet and I'm perfectly able to work for what I want.'

'I'm sorry. I should have told you. I didn't understand until I saw the woman at the wedding and I didn't like to go on about it. Now suddenly it seems important.'

'It doesn't matter.'

'Do you love someone else?'

Sep moved about, embarrassed. 'Love's not that easy.'

'And does she still work at Black's Foundry?'

'She fell in love with David Black. He's one of those bastards who has everything. I couldn't look at his parents at the wedding, they're such lovely people. His bride is beautiful, he's educated and . . .'

'You hate him?'

'Oh God, yes.'

They both laughed.

'He could have had Maddy if he'd wanted her,' Sep said. 'She would have married him.'

'I have a feeling it would have been a disaster. She's so strong and independent, is she not, and the Blacks strike me as traditional people? Why don't you go and see her?'

'I daren't. Every time I do see her she betters me and then I feel stupid. I don't think she cares about me any more at all. I'm afraid to try again.'

'You have nothing to lose,' Jonas said.

Sep couldn't go back to Durham again, not for that reason anyway. He told himself that he had asked Maddy Grant to go away with him twice and she had refused twice. The second time he could understand why she had done it to a certain extent, but both times he thought that if she had loved him she would have left regardless. He would have done that much for her.

He told himself there were plenty of young women in the area, surely some of them would be happy to go dancing of a Saturday night. The trouble was that he was seen as rich. It was ridiculous really, he thought, the opposite problem he had had with Maddy. He did not want to get involved with any of them and so he tended to stay away.

He got used to staying at home, there was so much work to do there seemed no time for anything else. Now that Mary and Jonas had gone he was completely alone.

Maddy had given up hope. David was married and the other men around her did not please her. She was beginning to think that she would go on as a spinster until she died. It was not so bad, she had come through the war, she had proved how useful she was by being at the foundry all that time and she now had a lovely home to go back to with her mother and Bert, her own room, good food, expensive clothes and she had learned to drive and bought herself a little car.

She loved having her independence. She looked at married women with small children and thought that she did not envy them and then she went down the dale to work. She liked being important at the foundry, being the only woman there, and David spent more time with her than he did with his family. She tried not to think that night after night he went home to Ella and that they had a child and then another. It was stupid to envy other people, you did not really know what their lives were like.

David's father's health continued to deteriorate and she was not surprised to learn that he was taken ill in the night and shortly after that, under Iris's nursing – she had been a Queen Alexandra nurse during the war – he flourished for a while and then Iris came into the office one day, running, and Maddy knew that Mr Black had died. After that she wanted to be there for David, he needed her help, and she liked being able to help him.

He was perfectly capable of running the business without his father, he had taken most of the responsibility for so long, but she was glad to help. David's mouth was sometimes white with the strain of having to run the business by himself and she was aware that Ella, his wife, knew nothing of such things and sometimes during the long afternoons they would both sit in his office, drinking tea and talking over the problems. These were her favourite times.

There came an evening, however, when he asked her to have dinner with him. They had had a lot of problems, the offices had burned down and new ones had been built and records were lost and they were both very overworked, but he had never before asked her to go out with him while his wife and children were waiting for him at home. She knew that she ought to have refused but somehow, just this once, she couldn't help herself.

She wasn't dressed for going out to dinner but she managed, and he took her to the County Hotel. Maddy was very impressed. She had been to the County before but only for tea and the dining room there was so neat, with perfectly starched tablecloths and shining cutlery.

The white wine was cold and tasted like gooseberries and the meal was all lemon and cream, chicken, grapes, a lemon soufflé but it was more difficult than she had thought it would be. Many times she had imagined she and David sitting across a table from one another eating dinner but it had not been like this.

They usually talked about work but it seemed silly here and she was searching her mind for something safe to talk about and she couldn't think of anything. His wife and children were off limits and she could not think what she and David had in common other than the office.

He asked her about her family. Maddy lied, telling him they had been farmers when in fact they were nothing of the kind. Her family had been very like his, and she told him that she had sisters and that was not true either. She was nostalgic about the house but brief, she didn't want to get into that, and afterwards they fell into silence.

They were rescued by music, it filled the silence, and he asked her to dance. Here again she had imagined so often being in David's arms, but when they danced it didn't work somehow. She felt awkward and thought that he should not have been there. Stupidly she cared about what his wife would think. It was not right and she had never done something which was not right before. Ella had married David and borne his children and they had a life together. She and David had an office together. She wanted to go home.

Rather more vocal than usual after the wine David said, 'I wish you wouldn't go.'

Maddy felt even worse then and wanted to get away. She just wished to get into her little car and go home, back to the dale where she belonged. She should have gone sooner, she should not have given him the impression that she wanted to do this. She had thought she loved David, now she knew he was her boss, it was her work she loved. She was very fond of him and had thought she would do anything for him, but it was not so.

'I must. My mother and Bert they worry about me and I didn't let them know I would be late.'

'Of course you must go,' David said.

He drove her back to the office, he kissed her on the cheek and Maddy had never been so thankful to climb into her little car and drive away. She did not go far. The tears coursed down her cheeks and ten minutes out of Durham she stopped the car. There she stopped the tears. She liked David Black but did not love him. He was not part of her life in the dale and never would be.

She drove home rather too quickly for comfort. Bert came into the hall.

'We thought something had happened to you,' he said.

'Nothing's happened to me. I had to have dinner with my boss.'

'Work again,' he said. 'You do too much.'

Maddy went into the sitting room where her mother and Bert had been sitting on the sofa, chatting. It was a lovely room, her mother had furnished it with Bert saying, 'Oh, lovely, Rose,' even when he didn't agree. He was the best man in the world, Maddy thought, glad to be back among them again. She didn't mind going out from here but she needed always to come back.

Sep had gone to a dinner in Durham with other pit managers and was staying at the County Hotel. The dinner was in a private room. He was late in getting there but was in time to see Maddy walk in with David Black and move towards the cocktail bar. Sep had not given himself much time but he found it difficult to go on with what he was doing as he watched them.

He couldn't concentrate. Sep knew David Black was married and had two children and here was Maddy having dinner with him. Later he saw them dancing slowly, close together with the soft music all around them. So that was it, he thought, she really did love David Black and was having an affair with him.

It must have been going on for years. Had David Black married his wife while he was having an affair? Was it that long standing or was it that he had married one woman and then discovered he had a desire for another woman and since he wasn't supposed to could have that one as well?

It didn't seem right somehow. Sep did business with David Black and he didn't seem the sort of man . . . His thoughts trailed away. Lots of men did the same, most of them did, especially men in business who had status and influence. David Black had a reputation to maintain. He was hardly living up to it taking his secretary to dinner and dancing, Sep thought. People would notice. He had.

He told himself it was nothing to do with him, but he couldn't get it out of his mind. Worse still there was a meeting the following day after breakfast to which several local businessmen had been invited and David was one of them. Sep could hardly bring himself to speak to him and David must have noticed it because when they streamed out of the room into the bar for lunch David came over to him.

'Is everything all right, Sep?' he asked.

Sep turned, smiling, from the bar.

'Why, yes, of course,' he said. 'Would you like a drink?'

'I really would. Things have been very difficult lately.'

'Have they?' Sep looked keenly at him.

'How was the dinner last night?'

'Fine,' he said and then, could not resist. 'How was your dinner,' and then David saw, he could tell.

'Ah. You were here?'

'Yes.'

'I've been having one or two problems lately. You may

not know but the offices were burned down and we've spent a lot of time building new ones. A great many records and important papers were lost and . . . Maddy has worked so hard and done so much . . . You used to be very friendly with her, didn't you?'

Sep could have hit him. Somehow he hated her name on David's lips. He had imagined David would call her Miss Grant or at the very least Madeline, it was too close, too intimate. He didn't reply. The whisky and soda arrived. He handed a glass to David while wanting to push it into his face or at least pour it over him.

David took it and thanked him.

'I remember years ago when we were all very young she came into the office crying and you were . . . you were leaving. I didn't know who you were.'

'I asked her to marry me.'

'Right,' David said and didn't look at him.

'Things were in a bad way. First of all I asked her to leave Sweet Wells with me but she wouldn't because of her mother and then I asked her to go to Northumberland with me when Jonas offered me a decent job but she wouldn't. I think I'm beginning to see why now.'

David did not try to look innocent, he did not even look down or away. All he said softly was, 'I don't think you are.'

'Aren't I?'

'It was dinner.'

'And dancing.'

'It was the first time.' David laughed in embarrassment.

'And what did you do afterwards?'

There was a spark in David's eyes.

'I went home to my wife,' he said.

'She must have been pleased to hear that you'd spent the evening with your secretary or didn't you tell her?'

'Things have been difficult,' David said. 'My wife . . .'

'Doesn't understand you.'

'There was somebody else.'

'Your wife had somebody else?' Sep was astonished.

'Not exactly, but I suspect this man meant a great deal to her when she was younger. There seems to be no evidence but . . . a bit like you now, I've let my imagination run off with me.'

'You looked to me like a man who would have spent the night with her.'

'Maybe I would, but she stopped me before I had even given the matter thought.'

'She's been in love with you for years,' Sep said.

'I don't think she has or if she has it was because she had nobody else. She doesn't have anybody, you know, just her mother and her mother's husband. I think she's very lonely. Work doesn't fill all the gaps.'

'Oh, I do know,' Sep said.

David looked down at the golden liquid in his glass.

'How's Jonas?'

'He's in Greece.'

'I wish I was in Greece or some other bloody place that wasn't Durham,' David said bitterly.

'Me too.'

David drained his glass.

'Do you fancy another?' he said.

They were coherent over lunch but only just. It was a beautiful summer's day and after lunch when they should both have gone back to doing something useful, he to Northumberland and David no doubt to his office in Durham, they sat and drank whisky and soda well iced and smoked through the afternoon, outside on two comfortable seats and watched the river go by, the sun move until the shadows were long.

It was only mid-evening when David said, 'I've got to go,' that they made a move.

Sep didn't get up.

'David—'

'It's all in your head,' David said straight away. 'Why don't you do the bloody decent thing and ask her to marry you?'

'Because I'm frightened she's going to turn me down again.'

'And that's the worst that can happen? Hasn't it happened twice already? You must be getting used to it by now.'

'Bugger off.'

David laughed.

'What else have you to do?' he said before he left.

It was Saturday afternoon and Maddy was at home. She was bored. She had taken a long walk by the river that morning, but she was still restless. She went out. She walked about in the village streets and then noticed some activity going on up the hill towards her old home. She had been working hard lately and had not noticed anything, coming back mid-evening and caring nothing for any more than a meal and her bed. She thought the atmosphere in the house had been strained over the last few days, her mother and Bert looking at one another and not saying anything. She went back into the house.

'What's going on up the hill?'

They were drinking tea in the sitting room. Her mother looked down into her cup, Bert staring out of the window.

'Don't you want tea?' her mother said.

'Do you know anything about it?'

'I don't know what you're talking about,' her mother said.

Maddy walked out. She began to climb the hill briskly. She was feeling the kind of out-of-sorts feeling which could turn to anger. It did when she got close enough to see a dozen men working and worst of all Sep Ward standing in the middle of what had been the front lawn. Issuing directions if she could tell anything at all.

'What are you doing here?' she demanded as she went across.

Strange after all this time she felt so proprietorial about it. It was still hers, it was still the old Grant place to the village.

She told herself that she couldn't believe he was there but it was true.

'I'm pulling it down,' he said, matter of factly.

'What?'

He moved away, talking to some of the men, telling them what to do as though he belonged here, as though he had never moved away.

'What right have you here?' she said, going after him.

He ignored her.

'Why have you come back?'

He still ignored her.

'What are you doing in Sweet Wells after all this time and what are you doing telling people what to do in a place that has nothing to do with you?'

He looked at her and then he said again, 'I'm pulling it down.'

He walked away and Maddy was furious now. Why couldn't he stay where he was and answer her questions?

'Who gave you the right to touch anything here?'

He didn't answer that either.

'I wish you would just stand still for a minute,' Maddy said.

He complied and looked at her so that she couldn't look straight at him. She knew she couldn't govern her tongue so for a little while nobody said anything. He looked at the village so far below them and she breathed very slowly.

'Pulling it down?' she said.

'Yes.'

'All of it?'

'Just the bits that are falling down, not the house.'

He looked at her and she thought she saw a question on his face as though if she had only told him to he would have pulled the whole thing down there in front of her eyes.

She watched the workmen and the machinery.

'What are you going to do with it?' she said.

He didn't answer and she said, 'I thought your uncle owned the house.'

'I know you did.'

Maddy said nothing more. She stood there and watched for some time.

'Has he sold it?' It was the only thing she could think of and she had not realized how much being here would hurt, that despite everything that had happened here it was still her beloved home.

He didn't answer.

'I wish that you would talk to me,' she said, looking him straight in the eyes and glaring at him.

'Do you really?'

'Of course I do. What do you think I trudged all the way up here for?'

'Curiosity.'

'Why did nobody tell me?'

'Maybe they thought you'd react like this.'

'And maybe you just didn't tell anybody what you were doing, just like always. You do what you want to do regardless of anybody else.'

'He gave it to me,' Sep said.

She went on looking at him, though not glaring. He did not meet her eyes that time.

'Your uncle did?' she managed.

'Yes.'

Just like that, she thought. He had given her house to Sep.

'And what do you intend doing with it?'

'I intend making it the most beautiful house on earth,' he said.

She was amazed, not just that he should think such a thing, or that he should suggest it, but that anybody would have the nerve, the courage to do such a thing.

'I thought you weren't coming back here. Don't you . . . run things in Northumberland?'

'Not everything,' he said, almost smiling.

After that there was a long enough silence for her to remember where she was, to think how much she had loved this place when she had been little, how she had been born here, how when she was a child she assumed she would always live here and somehow when her father died that she too would die there, with her spirit leaving by the window and not going far. It had to be one of the most beautiful places on earth and yes, the house deserved to be rescued, but did it have to be him?

'Some awful things have happened here,' she said.

'Yes, well, if a place is inhabited long enough I suppose that's inevitable.'

She thought it was a sensible way to look at it, unemotional, manageable.

'A lot of good things,' Sep said. 'You lived here all the years of your childhood. You must have fine memories of it.'

He was right, they had built snowmen in the garden, toasted crumpets over the fire, her mother had taught her to bake in the big square kitchen and Maddy had spent hours reading to her mother in there while she ironed. Her father had read her stories in their big bedroom where he would sit on the bottom of the bed.

She had waited for him to come home in the evenings, in the summer she would run down the fields when she saw him walking up towards her and meet him in the long shadows. And her father had died here, a peaceful death.

She liked to think that his spirit had soared out of the window and was still there up on the tops, where the heather was purple in August, the fells were white in January, the sky was deep blue in June with nothing to impede its colour and the hedgerows were sweet with birdsong almost always.

She didn't say anything. She had a particular desire to throw her arms around Sep and hide, but she had never hidden away, never relied on anyone and it was too hard a thing to do now.

She turned brave eyes on the house. It already looked better, a big space cleared around it as though it might breathe more now, as though it was coming up from the ocean like a lifted wreck.

'It looks wonderful,' she said.

'Come inside.'

She held back. He waited for her and when she didn't move he said again, 'Will you come inside?'

Still she hesitated and then let go of her breath. She nodded.

She wished she had stayed at home, wished she had not had to make the decision.

She had a comfortable home life, it was nothing to do with that, it was something to do with generation after generation of her ancestors living here. It might be stupid, it must appear so to people who emigrated, to those who moved around a lot, but she felt close to her father here and for all those who had spent their last moments at Grant House.

Sep took her by the hand, very gently, and led her towards the front door and the garden, which was in ruins, became once again the place where her mother was down on her knees on a little mat, weeding and her father was coming in from the fields after walking.

Maddy stepped inside the front door and the hall was flooded with bright afternoon light. All the old furniture which they had left when they moved because they had no room for it and possibly no need was gone. None of the windows were boarded up and sunshine spilled like butter across the floors. The doors of the rooms were open and she peered into each one, the sound of her shoes echoing on the thick empty floorboards.

They walked into the sitting room.

'Oh, my piano.' She let go of his hand, moved over to it and lifted the lid but the keys wouldn't play and those which did let out a tinny noise. 'It's wrecked.'

A bumble bee was buzzing against the glass in the sitting room. Sep opened the window and let it out. Maddy went to look at the view. It went all the way down the long track to the village and many a time she had stood here as a small child, waiting for her father to come home in the afternoon from his office in Stanhope.

'I miss my dad.' She hadn't realized she had said it aloud, she never said such things, never expected anybody's sympathy.

'I know you do,' he said.

She had almost forgotten he was there.

'Would you like the house?' he said. 'I'll give it to you.'

She laughed in surprise and turned. His face was full of honesty, so open.

'Don't be silly,' she said. 'You can't go giving houses to people.'

'Why not? It's yours by right.'

'Nothing is anybody's by right,' Maddy said. 'Not in this world. Everything has to be paid for.'

'It's been paid for,' he said, 'over and over.'

She shook her head.

'You're so worldly,' he said. 'So brisk and objective.'

'Not about everything,' she said, moving away and feigning an interest in the room which she no longer felt, he had disconcerted her so much. She was remembering how she had felt about him when she was seventeen. It didn't seem like such a long time ago. How strange.

'You could always marry me,' he said. 'Of course that isn't a condition. I've asked you to marry me so many times now I've lost count.'

'Only once.'

'Was it? It feels like twenty times.'

'You asked me to run away with you the first time. And the second time.'

'And now I'm asking you to run back. That, at least, is new, you've got to admit.'

'I'm an old maid.'

'We could soon put paid to that,' he said in a way that made her blush and move away even further. When she said nothing he said, 'You can have the house anyhow. I'd like that. If you don't want to marry me now I'm going to go away.'

'I thought you were managing the mine up . . . wherever it is you are. You couldn't do that if you moved back here.'

'There are mines here. There are businesses that people still run themselves. I think I could do anything.'

'I think you probably could too.'

'And I wouldn't object if you wanted to keep on working for David Black, even though I'm as jealous as hell.'

'There's nothing for you to be jealous of.'

'Isn't there? I think you've always been just a little bit in love with him.'

'Not nearly as much as I was ever in love with you,' Maddy said, surprising herself. She tried to get away then, wished the words unsaid, she felt so vulnerable, all the defences gone and it was not something she had done before and not something she thought she could ever feel good about.

He held her very gently.

'Were you really?'

She shook her head.

'Oh, go on. Tell me just once more and I won't bother you again.'

'But you'll give me the house anyway?' she said, not looking anywhere near him.

'It's yours.'

'Well, then . . .' She finally looked bravely somewhere near his face though her lips trembled. 'I want you to stay here with me.'

'Holy hell,' he said, 'you nearly made it,' and she laughed because he was right, she had almost told him that she loved him. She felt sure she would manage it later, when they went down the hill towards the village away from the house.

The people who had lived in the house seemed to always be a part of the dale and anybody who had ever been happy there was still there in some way, the best way, it was changed because of them and the same because of them and it went on. As evening fell they walked back down to the village together and the men went home and the sheep went on grazing until dark and the old cart horses further over were drinking from the stream.

The house was waiting to begin again, it only needed her to be there.

'And we'll buy a piano,' he said.

'I would like that more than anything,' Maddy said.

Books used for Reference and Information

Alexander, Les. *Seaham, A Town At War*, Lighthouse, 2002.
Arthur, Max. *Forgotten Voices of the Second World War*, Ebury Press, 2005.
Bader, Douglas. *Fight for the Sky, the Story of the Spitfire and Hurricane*, Pen & Sword Books, 2006.
Delaforce, Patrick. *Monty's Northern Legions*, The History Press, 2004.
Gibson, Len. A *Wearside Lad in World War II*. Great Northern Publishing, 2005.
Levine, Joshua. *Forgotten Voices of the Blitz and the Battle for Britain*, Ebury Press, 2007.